Free Me

Kat Winters

ISBN: 978-1-7369343-0-2

Cover design by Kat Winters

A dedication...

Where to begin?

How about we start with you!
This goes out to you!
Thank you for being here today!
Not just holding this book but breathing and giving life a chance!
This goes out to the boys and girls and everyone in between still
finding their way!
To the boys and girls and everyone in between who know who they
are, no matter what people say!

This goes out to the parents, trying so hard to understand!
This goes out to the parents who need a reminder in unconditional
love!
This goes out to the ones who've loved me,
The ones who fight for me,
Who taught me family is not defined by blood!
Who taught me kindness is mandatory for all!

This goes out to those who helped me.
To all those who cheered me on in the comments
To the girl with a heart so big she can't keep it in
To the girl who stood by me from the first "Hello"
To the girl who's got so much passion, it shoots out of her and into
me like electricity!

This goes out to you

Because you are here, and you are loved

You are valid and beautiful and worth it

Don't ever change, because this is for you!

Disclaimer

This story contains graphic and triggering content such as: *eating disorders, verbal abuse, emotional abuse, hate crimes, self-harm, suicide, homophobia, conversion therapy, and hate speech*. If you cannot handle one or more of these topics, please do not continue reading. No story is worth harming your mental health.

The Beginning

Take a moment and think about your high school years.

How many of you can remember countless times you tried to find yourself? How many of you also remember it being pushed aside by countless people saying, "You're young, you don't know what you're talking about," or my favorite, "It's just a phase"?

Nothing has changed. I honestly don't know if it ever will.

The only difference between the generations is that as time goes on, there's more to push aside. Now we have so many people in high schools trying to express themselves in new ways and having every attempt disregarded by at least one person. Unless it's a test with a perfect score, most parents will push it aside or only half listen.

I understand the constant pressure of being a teenager where no one can accept your choices and the ways society's changing. And like a lot of people, I let it control me, I let it hide me. I let fear and pressure keep me a captive within myself, well, at least until that year.

Senior year. Pretty much a bottomless hell hole without any emotions and personal growth involved. You have your schoolwork, teachers, finals, graduation, college, and that's not taking into account friends, dating, sports, clubs, prom, and all the other countless high school dramas there are. Why not throw more fuel on the fire? Maybe the smoke will kill us faster.

I'm Joshua, and I turn 18 in July. I have an awesome mom and dad who work hard and love me. I also have a sister a grade below me who I can't imagine life without. I've only had one girlfriend, and I never did anything more than kiss her. I'm taking a few AP classes and usually hang out with my family on weekends that I'm not working. Oh, yeah, and to top it all off...

I'm gay.

Only my sister knows. It fucking sucks.

The one girlfriend I had back in my freshman year was great, she was pretty and smart and always made me laugh. I met her when I signed up for the school paper and I thought I really liked her. I just never understood why I didn't feel anything when I held her hand or kissed her. She dumped me a few weeks after Christmas break because she thought our relationship was one-sided and I wasn't putting in any effort. My sister got a kick at how dramatic she was, honestly so did I.

After that, I felt different. Almost free, but not quite there. I spent the rest of the school year confused and unsure of what to think or feel. It was only after school got out for the summer that I started to understand.

Arriana, my sister, convinced me to help her sneak out to a party one of my classmates was having to celebrate the end of school. After some bribery, I agreed to go, and things got a bit out of hand.

While Arriana was having fun, I decided why not try to be social. There were enough people there for that, even if most of them were blind drunk. I ended up talking with this guy who I guess turned out to be the friend of a brother of a dude at the party or whatever. He was great. He was in college and as we were talking he asked me if I was straight.

"What do you mean?" I mean, what else could I be? His deep chuckle was drowned out by the painfully loud music and drunken laughter around us.

"Do you do chicks, or do you do dudes?"

"I haven't really done either I guess, the most I've done is kiss a girl."

He looked at me funny for a few minutes before looking around the crowd and grabbing my arm. "Come on, I want you to meet someone."

I followed close behind him as we pushed past the crowds of teenagers, at one point I almost lost him in the insanity of it all. I ignored the close contact and awkward dancing as I brushed past, trying not to knock anyone's cups out of their hand. We entered the back yard and came up to a small group of people who looked about the same age as the guy who brought me out here. They seemed to have formed their own bubble outside the party. At least they could probably hear themselves think. The music was still loud, but I was thankful to be out of the chaos.

"Look what the cat dragged in, who'd you bring us this time Ty?"

A girl who was at least six feet tall sat down on a planter with her legs spread and her chin in her hand. I watched her down the contents of her cup and put it down with a proud grin.

"I personally think this little guy, whatever his name is, needs a little help understanding what all is out there. I asked him if he was straight and all he said was 'what do you mean', like come on."

Their eyes went wide with shock as they looked at me, the same girl as before looked me up and down and dropped her head. "We're doomed," she said.

"What am I missing?" I asked, looking around as if I had missed some big neon sign.

"Do you think people can only be straight, kid?" The guy named Ty sat down next to his friends and stared at me.

"No, I know that some people aren't. I guess I just don't see what you mean. I've never been with a guy, why wouldn't I be straight?"

They burst out, cackling as one of them stood, bringing attention to the fact that I couldn't tell if they were a boy or girl. "What do you think I am?" they asked.

"I don't know, I can't even tell if you're a dude or not." I shrugged my shoulders in surrender.

"I'm transgender. I was born Lola, but I never felt secure in my own skin. I felt like a boy so I'm in transition to become one. Now, I'm Liam and it changed my life. Sandra over there is bi, she's not as picky about who she's with, she's attracted to both men and women. Ty is as straight as a bendy straw and has tried to take Tommy home countless times even though Tommy is asexual and doesn't want to get jiggy with it. I'm also pan meaning I couldn't care less what's in your pants or how you identify, if I like you I like you."

I looked them all over and realized just how similar they all looked. They had these huge differences between them, but they seemed just like every other person I had ever met.

"How do you figure out stuff like this about yourself? How do you decide you want to be a guy or want to do a guy?" I sat down, trying to wrap my head around the insanity I'd just been exposed to.

Sandra, the tall one, looked at Liam and snickered. "I think you explained it a little too fast. The poor kid's brain is going to short circuit. Look kid, it's about how you feel, it's who you are. It's the kind of thing that you try to understand most of your life, and usually, it *is* confusing. How do you think I felt when I felt hot kissing both guys and girls, I thought I was a freak. Ty almost had his parents send him to a shrink when he couldn't figure out why he felt nothing with girls."

I looked at Ty and watched him look down in embarrassment.

"My girlfriend dumped me a few months ago," I admitted. "I felt relieved. I felt nothing with her. Every time she kissed me I felt awkward and numb to it."

Sandra looked at Tommy, who looked at Liam before they all turned to Ty. Ty sighed.

"Ok, we need another gay dude because he's cute and all but I'm sick of being the experiment." They all chuckled before Ty came up to me and shrugged. "You at all curious to try and kiss me? I won't kiss you if you don't want me to."

I felt my stomach do flips, and I started sweating. Yet the nerves didn't feel bad or scary. It was more like I was nervous because I was excited. I glanced back at the others, then nodded.

Ty smirked before leaning down and pressing his lips to mine.

His lips were rough, unlike my ex who always had soft lips. Kissing him tasted different, too. My mind raced as I fell deeper into this kiss and realized I liked it. My heart raced and I felt myself vibrate.

Ty backed away and grinned back at his friends. "I think he gets it now."

They all asked me how I felt, but I couldn't find the words to explain it. Liam sat next to me and nudged me with his shoulder.

"That's what a kiss *should* feel like. It's supposed to knock you off your feet and leave you speechless, that's how you know it meant something, and you felt something real. The stomach flutters and sweating palms and shuddering, those are all the feelings you should get when you're attracted to someone."

"How do I know it wasn't a fluke?" I asked. "Maybe I just wasn't attracted to my ex. I could be like Sandra, right?"

"Yeah, for sure, you need to keep searching for yourself and find out where you stand. And whatever you decide you are is cool, because it's your life and you should live it honestly. Whatever label you use, whoever you love, you're valid. Don't let anyone tell you differently."

I looked over at Ty and started to blush, and I realized I was looking at him the way my ex looked at me.

I stood up and told them I had to go but that I appreciated

them trying to help. They wished me luck as I took off to find my sister to beg to go home. I found her dancing like a maniac and offered her a week of chocolate to go home.

After a thirty minute walk home, Arriana went straight to bed and I hopped on my laptop and searched what it meant to be gay. Some of what I saw scared me, like stuff people were posting about how being gay was an abomination and those who engaged in homosexuality would burn in hell. Other stuff though, comforted me and made sense, like reading the many stories of people finally feeling confident after discovering they weren't broken, just different.

I didn't sleep that night. I searched for hours before I finally felt secure.

That was how I discovered I'm gay.

I told my sister the next day because I was too scared to tell our parents. She hugged me and said she thought it was cool and was happy I felt safe enough to share it with her. It was the first summer in a while that I didn't feel like something was suffocating me. The first summer I felt like I really understood myself in the way a person should. By the start of my sophomore year, I knew without a doubt that I identified as gay, but I couldn't bring myself to admit it to anyone but Arriana.

Still trapped, but freer than I was before. It was a start.

August, Senior Year

Three years since I discovered I'm gay, and still only my sister knows. My parents are oblivious, thanks to my genius deflection.

Three years of my dad getting on me about when I'm going to bring a nice girl home, and my mom yelling that I shouldn't rush, that the right girl will come when the time is right.

Yeah, let's see how that works out.

The first day of my last year of high school is tomorrow, August 19th, and honestly, I think I'd rather dive into a pit of venomous snakes.

Living in Waco, Texas isn't easy. Or at least in my case. Waco can be awesome when I try hard enough to forget that I'm as straight as a spiral staircase. Even still being in the closet, I feel the pressure and how unwelcome it is to be gay.

Arriana is losing her mind with excitement and I wish I could relate. She has plans to meet her friends and go to Starbucks tomorrow morning. Today she's going with her friends to Richland Mall for a new outfit and to get her nails done and whatnot.

When she first found out I was gay, she thought it meant I was going to always want to shop with her and help her with her girl stuff, but the reality of the situation didn't meet her expectations.

I sit on my bed with a book in my lap and stare at my wall, trying and failing to distract myself from tomorrow. Instead, I've resorted to begging tomorrow to never come. I'm roused from my thoughts Arriana knocks on my door.

"Caira will be here in ten minutes, it's not too late to decide you want to actually look decent tomorrow. Maybe even get a haircut?"

"What do I get out of it?" I look at her and sit like a supervillain, stroking my chin.

"Get a haircut and get some decent clothes and I'll get you Chick-fil-A and Dippin Dots."

"Define decent." Arriana is less than thrilled with my laid back wardrobe, I never cared much about clothes and appearance, just comfort.

"A six out of ten on my scale."

"Deal!" I jump up and grab my shoes, phone, earbuds, and wallet. My sister knows me too well.

I walk out of my room to find mom "folding" at the foot of her bed as she pretends not to eavesdrop. She's been begging me to get out of the house all summer, it's just been harder for me as it gets harder to hide such a big part of myself.

"Josh! Honey, you're out of your room!" She jumps up and darts toward me. "Are you going with your sister to the mall? It could be fun, you might even see your friends there."

"Yeah, I'm going," I shove my hands into my jean pockets and try to avoid meeting her piercing grey eyes. "She thinks I need a haircut and new clothes, but I just want food."

She darts to her desk, moving like lightning as she grabs her wallet. She hands me forty dollars with probably the biggest grin I've seen since Arriana and I were really little.

"I think she's right, you've just sat at home the past two months. You are such a good looking boy, and you're hiding it inside with your hair covering your sweet eyes and old clothes hanging." She pouts and puts her hand on my cheek.

"Mom, come on, I just wanted to chill this summer. I'm fine." When she doesn't seem convinced I try to give her a real smile. "Really, I'm fine."

I take her hand down and she draws her arms in close to her narrow shoulders.

"I worry about you Josh, something seems different. If something is going on you can tell me honey." She comes closer and pushes back her hazelnut brown hair. "I just want you happy again."

I bring her into a hug, only now realizing how things really have changed. She was so worried when I quit the school paper, pushed away my friends, and started spending all my free time at work or playing video games. Freshman year, I was maybe an inch taller than her, now it feels like I have a whole foot on her. Freshman year, I would have told her everything and did, now...

Now I just settle for small talk when I see her at home.

"I love you, mom, and as long as *you* love *me*, I *am* happy."

She pushes me back and wraps her hands tightly around my arms. "I will *always* love you, and don't you dare ever think otherwise. You will always be my little boy and nothing could ever change how a mom loves her babies."

God, I hope she's right.

I give her a kiss on the cheek and rush out to the living room to find my dad rummaging in his briefcase for his keys. Again.

I reach over to the small bowl on the counter and whistle to get his attention. As he looks up I toss him the keys.

"Thanks kiddo! I can never remember where I put the damn things." He clips them to the bag and stomps over to me, hauling me into his signature dude hug where he crushes me with his tall frame and broad shoulders. "You ready for tomorrow?"

"Are you?" My dad leaves for a business trip to San

Antonio tomorrow morning. He hates them, but he's damn good at them. He's been in insurance sales for almost fifteen years now and is gone almost every other week.

"No, I want to see you off to your final year of high school, not stuck on some stuffy plane for two hours. But I will promise you that I will be here for your graduation."

"Thanks dad, but I think you'd much rather be home when Arriana brings her prom date over."

His face goes stiff. "I'll be sure to leave the shotgun where you can get it. Make the twerp piss himself."

I chuckle as my sister comes out bouncing around. She looks like a chihuahua that had a shot of espresso.

"Caira is here, come on let's go before you change your mind!" She grabs my hand and yanks me away from my dad and out the door.

I see her so excited and can't help feel my heart warm. She tries so hard to keep me involved in life but I rarely give her the chance, and now her honey colored eyes are sparkling with joy. For the first time in months, I get to actually see her smile enough to show her dimples. She has my mother's physique, but her hair, eye color, and dimples came from my father.

Her grey knit dress hugs her carefully and bounces with her in her sparkly wedges. She's even wearing the earrings I got her for Christmas.

As we get into her friend's car, they all look at me in shock.

"You're actually alive? We were starting to think Arriana was in denial and you were rotting in your room." Her friend Tempe looks at me in awe as she chews her bubblegum.

Arriana smacks her as we leave. Tempe has never had a filter. She once asked me if my dick was broken and that's why I never went out on dates. I never liked Tempe around my sister. She met my sister at a party and got Arriana so drunk I had to hold her hair when she came home.

The short drive feels like forever listening to Caira and Tempe gaga over boys and talk about what their classmates have done over the summer.

Out of nowhere, for the first time since I met her, Tempe says something that catches my attention. "That idiot Cupcake got his ass handed to him outside of Walgreens last week. Dumb shit thought he could take on Conrad."

"Tempe, you really shouldn't call him that." Arriana cringes at the sound of that awful nickname as she fixes her shoe strap. "He does have a name, and honestly no one has the right to call him any names."

"Yeah right Arri, like anyone is going to give that fruit loop more than five seconds to punch him." Caira adjusts her poofy hair in her rearview mirror. "He should just move his perverted ass back to hell. It's sick, and people think how he lives is ok."

I see the wheels in my sister's head turn before she opens her mouth, "You know Caira, about sixty years ago people would have spoken similarly about you."

We all freeze, Caira's dark skin drains as her eyes shoot daggers at my sister.

"Are you seriously comparing me to him?" She takes on a dangerous tone, the kind that tells Arriana to choose her words carefully.

"Honestly Cee, it's just something to think about." Arriana keeps her head high as she ends the conversation.

I've never been more proud of my sister. She's always been big on embracing everyone but has never voiced it so openly until today.

Caira shifts in her seat, wrapping her delicately decorated hands around the steering wheel, puckering her lips.

I squeeze my sister's hand and let my lips turn up in an appreciative grin, getting a caring smile in return.

By the time we arrive at the mall, all has been forgiven between the three girls and they start excitedly going into shops, dragging me along into American Eagle.

The first hour is them shoving clothes at me to try on. Tempe and Caira try to put me in preppy, brightly colored stuff before Arriana comes in with colors and clothes more suited to me. I agree to a few new pairs of plain dark jeans and a bunch of shirts that Arriana liked. I sit there at the register listening to her going on about dip dye and heathered shirts and the colors when really, I just want to get these and get food.

After we leave, the girls shove all their bags of clothes and shoes at me while they strut into Chick-fil-A. I don't really go inside anymore. Arriana used to work there, but didn't agree with a lot of their beliefs, so she left and came to work with me at Church's Chicken.

I sit on a bench outside listening to music for close to twenty minutes, debating going into the nearby bookstore or GameStop to pass the time before Arriana comes out with lemonade and a spicy chicken sandwich for me. She grins as she sits next to me.

"We would be out of there, but Conrad showed up and you know Tempe is determined to conquer him like all the other guys in school." She looks so grossed out and I don't blame her. Tempe has slept with just about every guy in school. At one point there was a rumor she had brain damage that affected her sex drive.

"She does know that Conrad has a girlfriend right?" I ask. "Even if she is at a different school in a different city."

"I really don't think she cares." My sister shrugs as she snags my lemonade, she looks me over carefully. "Are you ok? Did Caira get to you?"

I shake my head. "No, she just reminded me why I try so hard to hide."

"I hate when people call Zayne 'Cupcake'. It's so mean." My happiness dissipates and she scoots closer. "But I'm really glad you came today, even with her commentary. I miss hanging out with you."

"Me too." I drag her in and kiss the top of her head. "I miss hanging out with you too. Now let's get your friends out of there before Tempe starts stripping for him."

Arriana chuckles and looks over to the nail salon nearby. She runs to tell the others that nails are on her today, and they come out quicker than I thought possible in heels.

I watch as they disappear into the salon and I settle onto the bench again. I start to people-watch, just passing the time when I sit up, stunned.

I see Zayne walking into the Hot Topic near the salon. His head stays down as he runs his hand through his pink, frosted hair. His eye is swollen and his lip split. He comes back out not even ten minutes later with a bag in one hand, his phone in the other, and a big plush toy of some blue creature with big ears and big black eyes. I think it's from some Disney movie, but that was never my thing. He stands there typing on his phone for a bit before leaving, getting dirty looks on his way.

I hate the fear that instantly instills in me. My stomach

clenches at the thought of people looking at my family that way because of me. I try really hard to push him and these thoughts from my mind, thinking of the new level of my game, or the new book releases to check out, maybe even writing my own fantasy world to escape this sick feeling... But I still think of Zayne. I still think of how much he suffers for his bravery.

I envy his courage, but not the consequences.

WELCOME BACK, PRISONERS

I wake up to my alarm blaring on my nightstand. Groaning, I smack the off button and roll onto my back. My eyes still feel heavy. I know I slept, but I still feel restless and exhausted. Every day, every step outside, I'm filled with anxiety and terror at the thought of being outed.

Last night, all I could think about was Zayne and what he went through with Conrad at Walgreens. All night I was just seeing them fighting, and Conrad landing most of the punches as Zayne sat there trying to defend himself as the blood dripped off of him. I see Conrad and his tool friends yank on Zayne's pink hair, yelling at him and calling him "cupcake", "abomination", "vile", "sinner".

All night I saw that happening to me.

I sit up and rub my bare chest, trying to wipe away the sweat, when I see that Arriana has been in my room and took the liberty of picking clothes for me. I only know it was her because my mom would have waited in my room until I woke up.

I scoot myself over to the foot of my bed and stretch as I

stand. I can almost touch my ceiling.

I pick the clothes off my chair and look them over, scratching my newly cut hair. Arriana picked out a blue shirt, the short sleeves a darker blue than the torso, and a pair of dark jeans with a faded design. I guess she could have picked worse.

I get dressed and slip on my shoes. I should shower after all my sweating but I just don't have the energy, plus I know my mom will be in soon to get me up for breakfast.

My door opens as I debate getting back in bed and pretending to be sick, probably wouldn't work on the first day though.

"Honey," mom's gentle voice fills the room, "I made your favorite for breakfast."

I give a tired grin. "Thanks mom. I'll be out in just a minute."

The corners of her mouth drop and her cheeks stiffen as she drops the dish towel in her hand and comes over to me.

"Are you alright?" She puts her hand on my shoulder as I sit on the bed, "You look like you were up all night, do you feel sick?"

I shake my head and rub my forehead. "No, just nervous about today I guess. This is a very important school year, graduation and then college."

She gives me a half smile and runs her hand over my hair. "You'll do great, you always do. I don't think you or your sister have ever gotten lower than a C+ in anything."

"Thanks mom."

She kisses my temple and leaves for the kitchen.

I grab my bag and shove my two new folders my mom insisted on buying and a random handful of pens inside. I hesitate to put my journal in there, I'm always afraid someone will find it, so I hide it under my binders, books, and laptop.

I've had that journal for a little over a year now. It's where I write down all the things I want to say about being gay but don't. Every coming out speech, every comeback to the awful comments I hear, every argument to defend my sexuality. It's where I write down all my random thoughts and feelings, stories of fantasy worlds where no one is afraid to be themselves, statistics and random facts that occupy my mind, and all the useless nonsense I can find. It's my solace.

I sling the worn-out backpack over my shoulder and walk down the hall. Dad is already gone, but Mom is still bustling around the kitchen. She must hate that Arriana isn't here for her to fuss over and feed. Arriana, like a weirdo, would prefer Starbucks over our mom's breakfast.

I sit at the bar counter as my mom reveals a plate with thick cut bacon, home-style hash browns, and sunny side up eggs.

The joy on my face becomes visible as she puts up a bowl of dark oatmeal, filled with syrup and brown sugar.

I look at the clock and see that I still have forty minutes before first period starts, giving me enough time to eat and bike to school. I devour most of my food in less than fifteen minutes, not realizing how hungry I was.

I save my oatmeal for last, hoping it'll give me a boost before I leave. As I dig my spoon in, my mom pushes a plastic baggy in my direction and a ten dollar bill.

"Real breakfast for your sister, and money for food." She beams as I shovel the pure sugar of my food into my mouth. "I already snuck her money in her bag."

"You know we only need like half that right? And she probably ate with her friends." I wipe my mouth and slide the money and bag off the counter.

"Nothing she eats at Starbucks will qualify as breakfast in my mind. Go brush your teeth and get going. You need to find your locker and classes, maybe even see your friends."

What friends? It's hard to maintain a friendship when all you think about is what'd they would think if they knew the truth.

I scrub my teeth so hard in frustration that my gums bleed. I pop a piece of gum in my mouth hoping to mask the taste of the blood.

Giving my mom a kiss goodbye, I mount my bike and peddle for a short ten minutes and lock my bike on the rack when I arrive at the front gate.

Everyone comes flooding through the doors, some look excited and proud while others look like they still want to be in bed. My sister and I are on opposite ends of that spectrum. Seeing her come in with the largest grin proves my point.

I hand her the sandwich my mom made her and she sighs. "Thanks, I did feel bad for missing breakfast," Arriana says.

I take in her perfectly planned outfit and try to absorb some of her excitement and positivity. All I get is her clothes, her tiny, floral slip dress with her black cut-out heels that match the delicate black flowers on her dress. Her hair is flowing as she has two braids from either side of her head meet in the back and let out into the rest of her straight hair, auburn hair.

"You look really nice Arriana, I mean it," I gently push against her shoulder as a subtle, pink blush appears on her cheeks. She tries not to show how nervous she is for the year, or how self conscious she is, but I know, and I know how much she needs reassurance.

"You aren't so bad yourself..." Her bubbly attitude disappears as we enter the door and her eyes are drawn toward the lockers. I follow her gaze.

Conrad.

He has Zayne pressed up against the lockers as his no-good drones help hold Zayne still.

Zayne has never been strong, his arms fight against the force being put on them, but they barely move at all. He almost kicks Conrad in the shin, barely missing and getting punched in the gut for it.

"You really are a delicate, little cupcake, aren't you? Can't even man up and fight back! God, you really are stupid to show up this year, we all figured you'd be in some camp or dead by now." Conrad smirks and pushes Zayne back into the locker one last time before telling his friends to drop him.

He falls to his knees and holds his stomach. They kick his backpack as they walk away and call him names.

Once the crowd clears, Arriana darts over to help him pick up his stuff. I follow close behind.

She helps put his stuff back into his bag as I help him get steady on his feet, he cringes with every move.

"You don't have to do that," he mutters to my sister who smiles and keeps picking up his stuff.

"Trust me, nothing you say will stop her," I whisper to him, causing him to let out a small snicker. I see his split lip up close, the dried blood has formed a dark, scab.

"If you want, I can help you get to the nurse." Arriana lifts the backpack and carefully holds it out as he takes it from her hand. The first bell rings.

"No, it won't fix anything, I should get to class. Thanks though," He gives a forced smile. The same as me.

Zayne makes it halfway down the hall before I kick myself and call out to him. "What class?"

"Physics." He still holds his stomach as he turns to see me catch up to him.

"Me too, I'll walk with you." I try not to look excited, try to hide how nervous I am. I want to be close to him, I want to tell him I get it, but I can't find the words.

"I'd like that. I'll let you walk in first so no one gives you any crap for it."

I almost think it would make things easier if they did, having to get used to it.

The walk is slow as Zayne tries not to stress his bruised stomach. He gives me a small head start, maybe thirty seconds to get in the classroom before him.

My teacher, Mr. Roe, looks over his glasses and clicks his tongue at me. "Cutting it close, Mr. Notes. Take an empty seat."

I find a seat in the back and drop my bag on the desk not

long before Zayne comes in. Conrad cackles and high fives his friends when he sees him struggle.

"Hush now." Mr. Roe adjusts uncomfortably on his desk. "Mr. Daveen, seeing as today is the first day I won't mark you tardy. Don't make it a habit though. Find a seat."

"Yes sir." Zayne nods his head and starts walking. I now notice that the only open seat is next to me.

"Probably not the only time he's calling someone 'sir'," I hear Conrad mutter to his friends. "Sick perv."

Zayne squeezes his bag as he walks to the back toward me. He looks at me hesitantly as he cautiously climbs onto the stool next to mine.

He lowers his head and mutters, "so much for helping you avoid shit."

I feel my hands sweat as I reach into my bag for my journal and a pen. I watch Zayne eye it curiously as I open to the last half-filled page and wiggle my pen.

Who's the pervert? The one who dares be honest about himself, or the one who assumes he's having crazy kinky sex?

Zayne chuckles as he reads my writing and grabs a pen to write on his hand. He writes fast and shoves his pen in his pocket as Mr. Roe starts talking.

I look at his hand.

Maybe we're all pervs.

I smirk and stare up at the board, not hearing a single word as Mr. Roe rambles on about requirements to pass and the syllabus. I spend most of the class glancing at Zayne. I even catch myself wanting to touch his hair.

The pastel pink tips make it look so soft. If it weren't for the constant beatings, most of him would probably be soft.

I carefully tear a piece of paper out of my journal and scribble a note and slide it under his hoodie sleeve.

Hang out tonight? 10 o'clock?

He looks surprised, his sagging eyes get wide and his mouth hangs open. He looks up and smirks, giving a subtle nod before writing on the paper.

Crestview park. Be there at 10.

I try to hide a smile as I slide the paper back into my journal and watch the New School Year PowerPoint on the screen.

Tonight I might actually sleep more than two hours. Tonight, I might actually feel understood.

Tonight might actually feel right.

INCOGNITO

I sit in bed listening to Mom talk on the phone with Dad until after nine and I start to wonder if I'll be able to sneak out or not. I didn't even tell Arriana that I'm meeting Zayne. All I told anyone is that I had a long day and wanted to go to bed early.

Mom didn't question it after seeing how exhausted I was this morning. Arriana gave me a suspicious side glance but shrugged it off.

Once the house falls silent, I slip on my shoes, shove my phone in my pocket, and slowly open my window. I climb out carefully and make my way to the front of the house. I wait until my mom's light goes out before mounting my bike and taking off. I check my watch. It's 9:38.

I try to keep a steady pace, but my need to sleep slows me down. What normally would only take ten minutes, takes closer to fifteen, cutting my arrival time close to ten o'clock. Zayne is already there sitting on the swing set.

His pink hair pokes out from under his hoodie as he slowly swings back and forth, kicking the ground as he swings.

"You know," I begin. Zayne's head jerks up when he hears me, "I could push you, get you more than two inches in the air."

He adopts this crooked grin as he leans over the side of the swing. "My hero."

As I walk behind him to sit on the other swing, I give him a quick push and he giggles. I don't think I've ever heard him laugh or seen genuine joy on his face. He came out in middle school, and the day he came out was one of the last days he really seemed happy.

"Do your parents know you're here?" He gives me a skeptical look.

"No, I snuck out my window after my mom went to bed. And I didn't sneak out for the reasons you think." His face doesn't change and my smile grows.

"I promise it's not because I'm embarrassed to be seen with you or because I'm doing this out of pity."

"Ok, then why? Why be out here with me?"

"I admire you."

His skepticism vanishes and his mouth drops open slightly as his eyes widen and his entire body relaxes. I can't read him, I want to know what he's thinking. His eyes search me, I think he's waiting for me to start laughing or say it's a joke. I think we're both waiting for the other to react, both of us need this but don't know what to do.

The silence stretches out farther and neither of us move. Neither of us knows what to do or say. We're both helpless in shock.

I watch as his lips dry out from his mouth hanging open. He is the first to move as he licks his lips and turns to the empty playground in front of us.

"Zayne, you live in a place that isn't going to express what I just said even though you deserve to hear it," I finally say. " You have the courage to own who you are and even when they beat you, tear you down, and belittle you, you don't give into them. It would be so easy for you to just give in to every beating, but you fight back. You could have dropped out or transferred schools and pretended to be straight, but you stay in the place you know and stay true to you. You have a lot about you worth admiring."

He looks over at me, jaw clenched and eyes shining. "I don't think you could grasp how much I needed someone to say something like that," he whispers. "And to top it all off, I can't figure out why you did."

I feel my heartbeat in my teeth, and my stomach fills with knots. I start to wonder if I'm going to puke. I sit there for a few minutes as I try to gain the courage to say what I came here to say.

"I...I admire you for having the strength to do what I still can't. I envy your ability to be honest about who you are."

His entire demeanor shifts, he straightens up and his face softens, after a few minutes of silence he says, "Are you saying that you're gay?"

I shrug, unable to find the right words. Saying *yes* doesn't feel like enough. "Only my sister knows. Every day something happens that makes me so badly want to tell someone else but I never seem to be able to. And... If I'm being honest, I think about you a lot; what you go through, how strong you are. I just really want to know you, I feel I can be honest around you, and I want to offer the same."

He shoots up from his swing, surprising me into standing with him. I don't know what I was expecting him to do or how I expected him to react but I wasn't thinking anything like this.

He comes up and jerks me into him, hugging me tightly. It softens me, my heart stops hurting, my body relaxes, and my stomach stops aching. I feel understood in a way I've never felt. It feels like someone finally gets it, it feels validating.

We sit there swinging next to each other for a couple hours, just talking. I tell him how I came to find out I was gay, talking about the party that summer, about Ty and his friends, and how terrified I was. We both admit researching was scary, seeing some of the awful things people would say about people like us. I find myself mesmerized as I listen to him tell his self discovery story.

"It was seventh grade, and I went to spend winter break with my cousin in Seattle. I had been struggling since the start of the previous year and my parents thought some time away might help. While I was staying with him, we went out to events and stuff, one of them was a LGBTQ+ support event a club at his school was holding. They handed out pamphlets with information on sexuality and gender identity and hotline numbers for people who were confused or having trouble accepting themselves. I talked with my cousin about it and the girl handing out pamphlets even though it all sounded so crazy. After he went to sleep that night, I used his house phone and called one of the hotlines, just trying to understand. I spent three hours talking to a rep, and after that call, it all fit. Why I always felt nervous in the locker room, why I never wanted a girlfriend, why I couldn't focus on anything, I finally understood."

"And then you came out at school, I had the flu that day. I saw you in the nurse's office waiting for your mom."

He tenses, "She wasn't happy that day. She hated that nothing was really done about it and hated I didn't talk to her first. She hated seeing me hurt, watching all these kids who were once my friends, kids who had been hanging out at my house just the day before, turning against me and acting like they never knew me. She felt so helpless and disappointed that she couldn't even tell me it would be ok, that she couldn't have mentally prepared us for this reaction because she didn't even know."

"What about your dad?"

"He... He struggles with it. I guess it's better than him disowning me and kicking me out but it's still really hard on us. He definitely treats me differently now, I can't imagine how he'd react to me bringing a guy home. It just feels like he doesn't know what to do with me anymore, if that makes sense. There are days I wish I was straight just for him."

I understand that, part of me wishes for the same thing, just to avoid hurting my parents and to avoid Arriana ever getting back-lash for who I am.

When I look and see it's almost one in the morning, I tell Zayne I need to head home, "You should too. Unless you plan on ditching your second day, we have to be up in the morning."

He grins, "Yeah, you're right. My mom is probably up waiting for me, I should go so she can at least sleep some tonight."

I hug him and hesitate to let go, I feel him do the same. I don't think either of us are used to a support system.

I bike home and quietly crawl through my window. Climbing into bed, I don't feel any pressure or fear.

I grab my phone and see texts from my sister.

I heard you open your window.

Where did you go?

Those are from over an hour ago, I hope by now she's asleep and elect to ignore her text.

I feel happy in a new way, happy enough that instead of sleeping I set up all my stuff for school including picking out one of the shirts Arriana got me. I organize my already hectic binders and prep to turn in the syllabi my mom signed.

By the time I lay down and actually close my eyes it's been almost an hour and I can feel the exhaustion luring me deeper into my mattress. I fall asleep, thinking of how Zayne reacted when I said I admire him, and all we talked about. As I delve deeper into sleep, my mind starts focusing on when he licked his lips, and how his hair barely peaked out from his hoodie.

Peaceful sleep.

BABY STEPS

I wake up to my alarm and look over to see the clothes I picked out have been switched for others. I check my phone and see Arriana has texted me nonstop for the past hour.

That shirt wouldn't match those jeans.

How are you still asleep???

I still want to know where you were last night

OMG how late does your alarm go off??

I drop my phone on my nightstand and roll out of bed to hop in the shower. I step in before the water heats up, hoping the cold will wake me up all the way. No such luck.

Fumbling into my clothes and shoving stuff into my backpack, I feel like a slug dragging through honey. It's weird, I barely slept, but it was the best sleep I've had in years.

I put my backpack on the bed as Arriana slips into my room.

"Ok, spill your guts. Where did you go? I was going to stay up and grill you, but I fell asleep. When did you get home?"

"Arriana, I'm still waking up, give me a bit. And keep your voice down." I wave my hand through the air at her and sit down.

When I see her, my heart sinks a little. Again, she's planned her outfit very carefully. Her skinny black jeans and pastel pink blouse, everything from the flower in her hair to her black flats is perfectly coordinated. But all I see is the pink.

"Zayne."

"Zayne?" she echos, surprised.

My mind goes back to last night and suddenly I'm wide awake. Even more so knowing I'll see him in first period. I think of how soft his hair looked, and how badly I want to touch it.

Arriana's eyes go wide, "No way!" She softens her voice to a whisper. "Do you like Zayne?"

"I don't know, we hung out last night and it just felt good, like I had someone who *really* understood. Someone who understood in a way no one else can, not even you."

She starts clapping and hugs me tight, and starts going on and on about how I should ask him out or get his number. I roll my eyes and head for the door. I smell breakfast and honestly, all I want is to stuff my face.

Arriana huffs as she follows me into the kitchen. Her

frustration dissipates when she sees Mom putting out plates of biscuits and gravy. We sit next to each other at the counter and praise our mother with our mouths half full.

Mom giggles and hugs us both. "I remember when you two were still in elementary school. You would always eat biscuits and gravy, every meal if you could. Now look at you, so darn big."

She babbles on some more, squeezing us tightly in her arms. My plate is empty before she lets us go. I leave to brush my teeth, then give mom a quick kiss on the cheek before darting out the door.

I mount my bike, taking off and getting to school faster than I ever had before. Even if I don't talk to him, I at least want to see Zayne, give him some subtle clue that I enjoyed last night and appreciated getting to talk so openly with him.

I walk through the door, half an hour still until class starts, looking over the mostly empty halls trying to find him. I dart to my locker and shove my backpack in there so I can go roam the halls looking for him.

Part of me wonders if I'm reading too much into all this, part of me wonders if he didn't care about seeing me again or not. It was just a conversation, just us talking through how we got here. It's not like we kissed or went on a date.

As I get closer to the Physics classroom I see him at his

locker. He looks exhausted, and like he's getting sick. He rests his head on his arm against his locker door, just standing there. I want to ask him if he's alright but then I see people walking down the hall behind him.

Conrad.

As Conrad passes Zayne he reaches out and drags his foot under Zayne, catching him off guard, knocking him onto his back on the floor. Zayne starts coughing.

"Uh oh boys, don't get too close," Conrad says snidely. "The fairy is sick. Probably got HIV or some shit. Be careful, he might give it to you."

They all snort snicker as Conrad grabs Zayne's backpack and throws it down the hall.

I kick myself, I tell myself to keep walking. But I can't.

Zayne starts to stand and tries to hold his ground, but Conrad starts building up to punch him. Before he throws the punch I step between them. I stretch out my arms to get as much space as I can between them, pushing Zayne ever so slightly into his locker for effect.

Conrad drops his fist. "What are you doing?"

"Dude, it's the second day. Can we have one day without bloodshed?"

"If the freak would defend himself and be a man, it

wouldn't happen as often."

I fight the urge to punch him, instead think about punching myself as I sit there with the perfect way to shut him up in my head.

"You know Conrad, if you're really worried about HIV then getting his blood on you isn't a good idea, but it's your choice."

His face pales as he and his friends take a few steps back.

I fight a smile. "You should go before any teachers show up. Keep an eye on your health."

Conrad and his friends take off. I turn to Zayne who has his head hanging low. He's sweating.

"Zayne? Are you ok?" I ask.

He shrugs. "Didn't feel well this morning. You didn't have to do that, you're lucky they didn't beat you up too."

"Stop, I'm not going to just let them attack you every day, especially when you look like you can barely stand up. I'm taking you to the nurse, and I'm calling your mom because I know you won't. What's her number?"

"Josh, seriously, I'm alright. It'll pass by the end of the day, it was just a rough night when I got home. I probably just ate something bad."

"Please let me take you to the nurse."

He looks up at me and sighs. Finally he agrees. I go to pick up his backpack with him hobbling behind me.

I get him to the nurse without incident, as Zayne insisted on the long, isolated path. The nurse greets us wearily. She was expecting this visit to be about a fight. I explain to her how sick Zayne is feeling while he lays down in her office.

After taking his temperature, which was at 101.8°, she goes to call his mom. While she's on the phone, I take out a pen and write my phone number on his hand.

"Text me, ok? I want to make sure you're alright."

He lights up and nods. I leave to let him rest while he waits for his mom to come pick him up. Right as I walk out of the office, the bell rings.

I don't want to be late, so I book it to Physics, making it to my seat with maybe two minutes to spare.

Conrad and his pals come in and see me sitting by myself in the back. To them it's a field day. Now they think they've accomplished something, now they think they have fuel to talk shit, even though I know fifteen minutes ago they were running scared.

"Lucky you, you got spared the torture and risk of sitting next to that creep for an hour," Conrad says.

I fake a smile and nod as I slide out my journal, wrapping

my arm around it and act like I'm working on something as I try to tune him out.

More like I'm being spared the torture of having to watch you torment someone sick.

I feel my backpack buzz in my lap. I whip out my phone and see a text from an unknown number.

Thanks for your help today. I want to make it up to you, I'll call you later :)

I let the corners of my mouth turn up as I save the number into my contacts. Mr. Roe comes in and starts talking about our first unit and asks to collect the syllabus. I spend most of the period texting Zayne and trying to make him feel better.

My mom makes some bomb cookies, I could bring you some tomorrow?

My mom has always loved to bake and cook, so it's very rare we don't have home cooked meals and bakes in the house. Usually my dad could eat all her cookies in an hour but with him gone, the rest of us can get to them.

Zayne's response comes quickly as we go back and forth.

You don't have to, I'm probably going to be at school tomorrow. It's just a fever

Until it's broken and you're feeling better you should stay home. I'll sneak out tonight and bring you cookies, sweets help everything

No joke :)

My heart skips a little as I put my phone away.

At lunch, I lure Arriana away from her friends to tell her everything and to beg her for help covering for me tonight. She gives a big grin and agrees excitedly. I, like her, can't stop smiling.

I spend the rest of lunch using my energy to do homework. The more I get done, the sooner I can "go to bed" and check on Zayne. Nothing can bring me down, until I see Conrad sit across from my sister and her friends.

Putting my stuff away, I make my way over to them. The look she gives me tells me that she needs help, but doesn't think it's a good idea for me to be there. I don't care.

I sit next to her and hug her. "What's up?"

She doesn't get a word out before Caira speaks up. "Conrad says you helped save him from catching something from the cupcake. Is it true?"

Arriana looks like she's going to cry of embarrassment.

"Yeah actually," I reply. "He has a really bad fever and ended up going home, hopefully he'll get better and no one else will get sick in the process."

They all look shocked by my response. I knew what they

were talking about, and they knew I knew. They can push if they want but I'll be damned if I play their game.

"I don't know, maybe he's not so bad," Tempe stares at Conrad, seductively licking a lollipop, "Maybe he just needs the right girl to...set him *straight.*"

They all start cackling and snickering, except me and Arriana. We sit there for all of lunch deflecting their commentary. It gets hard to hold my tongue and I start to feel my cheeks get warm. Arriana reaches over and holds my hand under the table, giving an understanding squeeze.

I spend the day on edge, but the knowledge of my trip to Zayne's place makes it better.

Coming home, I sit with my mom and help her clean the kitchen after dinner. She insists on going to bed early as she seems to be feeling unwell. I help her as much as I can before she heads for her room around seven.

I wait two hours before getting a bunch of cookies and telling Arriana to cover for me. She asks me to say hi to Zayne for her before I head out.

He sent me his address late in the day and it isn't super far, a little ways past school at the Sandstone Apartments. I try to keep calm and not rush, but I want to see him and know how he's doing. My mind keeps returning to his texts and his face when I gave him my number. My heart beats in my teeth as I force myself to peddle slower.

It takes a little longer than I originally planned given I tried to slow myself down to not look overly eager. I put my bike by the stairs to his unit when I suddenly feel sick.

I'm meeting his parents, I'm at his house. I think I might get sick. I know I'll get sick.

I build my courage and walk up the stairs, hesitating to knock on the door. Taking my chance with the split second I have of confidence, I ball up my fist and knock on the front door.

UNDERSTANDING

"You must be Joshua! Come in, please, you must be tired after your bike ride!" I'm greeted by wide eyes and a huge smile dragging me into the apartment.

I don't know how to react, so I just give a weary grin and stare. Her brown hair falls a little bit above her shoulders and her amber eyes shine like honey. Just like Zayne's.

She lowers her voice a bit. "Zayne's in his room. Thank you for taking him to the nurse's office. I didn't see him this morning, I had no idea he had a fever. He came home and wouldn't stop talking about you. He was so excited to spend last night with you and he wanted to text you as soon as he got home."

I feel myself fill with joy as her positive energy infects me. I see a door open behind her, Zayne comes out in a huge grey Neon Trees T-shirt and brick red sweatpants. His eyes seem heavy as he drags himself out the door and rubs his eyes.

"Mom, please don't scare him away." His voice is rough and raspy.

Honestly, it's hot. I'm so in over my head.

Zayne smirks at me, his eyes still hanging low. "Hey," he mutters as he leans back on his door frame. "Want to come sit down?"

I look at his mom, wanting to make sure she's ok with me in his room. She gives me a small nod and nudges me in his direction. Returning her smile, I walk in Zayne's direction. I try to hide how nervous I am, and how the sleepy look has me weak at the knees.

"You should relax dude," he pokes me lightly in the shoulder, "My mom won't bite. Maybe talk you to death, though."

He rolls his eyes as he drags his feet walking back to his bed. His room is pretty big, bigger than I expected. His bed is a mess of bunched up sheets and blankets in the far corner of his room. His nightstand has a lamp, an alarm clock, a box of tissues, his phone, and a couple random books. Across from the foot of his bed is a dresser with a TV, cable box, and Xbox on it. I look next to me at the desk by the door, the computer looks perfect and well kept but the rest of the desk is covered in pencils, pens, and paper with all types of things scribbled on them.

He sits on his bed and stretches his arms above his head.

"Were you sleeping? I didn't want to wake you up when you should rest."

He shakes his head and pats his bed. "I kept waking up anyway. It's hard to get comfortable when one second I want all the blankets and the next I want none of them."

I nod as I look at his tangled cement grey blankets. He still looks really sweaty. It doesn't look like anything has changed.

Slowly lowering onto the bed next to him, I pull out the cookies I brought and his eyes light up.

"No way! You weren't joking?" He snags the bag from my hands and starts cackling. It quickly turns to a coughing fit, making it hard for him to catch his breath.

"Are you alright?" I ask as he lays back on his mountain of pillows.

He shoves a cookie in his mouth and nods. "My mom thinks I have a cold. With my luck, everyone at school will think I killed myself or dropped out."

I look down at his blankets. I know he's right. If he's gone for more than three days, rumors will start to spread and make things worse.

I scoot closer, feeling my blood boil at the thought of how people will talk about him, "You know I'll defend you to any bullshit, I did it today and no one batted an eye, but at least someone can defend you."

"Do that too much and you'll get figured out faster than

you ever thought possible." He takes another cookie and sighs. "Ok yeah, your mom rocks at baking. I could die happy right now."

I shrug. "What are friends for? I can bring you more tomorrow."

He beams with crumbs all over his lips, "You could just give me the recipe. If you become my cookie dealer, you might as well move in."

I hear a door open at the other end of the apartment and see a big man with broad shoulders and black hair step into the living room. He looks at me on his son's bed and clenches his jaw. Assuming he's Zayne's dad, I stand up and take a step back out of respect. Nothing in his demeanor changes as Mrs. Daveen steps up to distract him.

Zayne appears in front of me, closing the door and ending my stare down with his dad. "Ignore him, he does that even if it's just me in here."

"You two really have issues huh?"

I watch him slump into his desk chair and start spinning.

"He says he's fine with it, but I think you can see why I don't really believe it," Zayne says. "The three of us haven't spent more than five hours in the same room together in maybe eight months."

I think that's why I haven't told my dad, I'm afraid of losing him. Seeing how Zayne's dad's behavior is affecting him is hard to watch, let alone experience.

Zayne bites his cheek and crosses his arms. I watch him start bouncing his leg, causing the fabric of his sweats to look like it's vibrating. He still has the cookies I brought, but now he can't even seem to look at them.

The door slowly opens as Mrs. Daveen comes in.

"How are you two doing?" She looks at her son, "Your dad went to go meet his friends, probably will be back late. Are you sure you don't want dinner? You won't get better if you don't eat."

"I'm fine mom, thanks." Zayne's head stays down.

Her face is soft and lips turned down. She looks worn down. It must be hard to be the mediator, trying to stay true to her son and her husband when they can never see eye to eye.

His mom leaves and he slumps over, putting his head in his hands. "I'm sorry, you shouldn't have to see all this. It doesn't help that I'm sick and I just want to yell at everyone."

"If you want to yell, I'll listen. I understand how it feels wanting to just get it all out." I sit down on his bed again and we just stare at each other.

"I just want to feel normal being me," Zayne finally says.

"My dad doesn't talk to me, my mom puts on a face, kids I used to call friends spend all day calling me names and telling me to kill myself. I just want it to all stop." He gets up from his desk and sits next to me. "The only thing in months that has felt normal is talking to you. You get it, no one else has ever understood before and I just...I don't really know how I feel about it."

My brain shuts off for a minute. I want him to understand how I feel, how much I want to be here for him. I don't want him to feel alone.

I reach over, putting my hand on his cheek, and lean in. The second my lips touch his, the energy changes between us. His body stiffens in surprise but he quickly relaxes and embraces my advance.

His lips are so much softer than I thought.

He presses his mouth harder to mine, the split lip scraping against mine. He scoots closer and puts his hand on my knee, my heart starts racing faster and faster. I take a chance and run my hand up from his cheek and into his hair, it's so soft and smooth I feel like I'm touching a pink, silky cloud.

"Zayne!" We hear his mom from outside the door and jump apart. "Do you and Josh want some lemonade?"

He squeezes his eyes shut, "No mom! We're good!"

I start to chuckle. He presses his lips into a thin line as he snorts to suppress a snicker, he leans over and presses his forehead to mine.

"I'm sorry," I whisper. "I should have said something before I just..."

He presses his lips against mine for a minute before pulling away with the biggest grin. "If we had all night, I would ask you to do it again."

I take his hand in mine. It feels right. I look over at his desk by the door, worried his mom will come in and yell at us when I see a small case next to his chair.

"What's that?" I get up and walk over to it, picking it up. It looks a little like a small guitar case, just curvier.

"It's a violin." Zayne stands up and shoves his hands into his pockets.

"Do you play?"

"Since I was ten." He looks embarrassed, pulling his arms closer into him and kicking a bundle of blankets at his feet.

"Could you play something for me?"

Zayne looks caught off guard, based on how the case is hidden I'm guessing his choice of instrument doesn't always sit well with people. "Maybe another time," Zayne replies. "I hate to say it, but you should probably go before my mom starts thinking you're moving in."

I hesitate and gently put the case back. "You're probably right, if my mom finds me gone she'll flip."

I reach for the door and he quickly pulls me back into another quick kiss.

"Call me later? Maybe we can set up a real date?"

I nod with a goofy grin before stepping back and walking out the door. His mom is standing at the kitchen counter as I walk out.

"Leaving so soon? I could drive you home if you'd like dear," she wipes her hands on her jeans as she rounds the corner of the counter.

"It's ok, Mrs. Daveen. I have my bike. It'll only take me twenty minutes."

She nods as she comes in to give me a hug, she squeezes me and gently speaks in my ear.

"Thank you for everything. He needs someone, someone who can be there in ways we can't." She pulls back, finally giving a real smile. "I think you'll be good for him."

I give her a nod, saying goodnight and heading out the door. As I mount my bike, I look and see Mr. Daveen sitting in an old station wagon in the parking lot. He sits there scribbling something on a notepad.

I watch for a couple minutes trying to figure out what

could be so important that he needs to hide in his car and lie about where he is. I wonder if he just wants to avoid Zayne, knowing another guy is in the house with him.

My phone buzzes.

Thank you for tonight...for all of it <3

I text back immediately.

I wish it didn't have to end. Feel better soon, I want to see you. Get some rest :)

I give one more glance to Mr. Daveen's car before I start pedaling home.

I stop at a crosswalk and text Arriana to open her window so I can get in and tell her everything. I can see my street getting closer and his house getting farther away. I want him closer to me, I want him better so I can see him at school everyday. I want him.

He wants me.

I quietly put my bike back and sneak to Arriana's window where she sits waiting. The questions start flying the second she opens the window.

"Can I at least get inside? I don't think you want me to freeze to death in the middle of my story."

"Then hurry up! I'm dying here, it's after eleven and I've been waiting forever to know what happened. Did he like the cookies?"

"Yes, it really seemed to help."

She pulls me inside and I flop on her fluffy white and rose bed. Her room is so much cleaner and organized than mine. Books and video games and journals are all scattered in my room, clothes in random piles... I should probably clean up. I probably won't.

After telling Arriana *everything* she starts gushing about how happy she is for us and how messed up everything is for people like us. I escape her grasp with the excuse of being tired.

"I'll bet you are," she winks before hugging me and sending me to bed.

I plug in my phone and read one last text from Zayne before shutting everything off. The small words on the screen make my heart skip a beat.

Goodnight...boyfriend.

Extra Large Order of Truth

It's been three weeks since Zayne and I kissed. We've spent almost all of our spare time together, going out when I don't have work, or hanging out on my break and going to his place after. Arriana has been great covering for me. She's spent a lot of time actually studying to cover for me leaving the house. While Tempe and Caira don't like her being M.I.A, Zayne and I certainly appreciate her efforts.

Zayne and I had gone to Dallas over the weekend and at a shop at one of the malls, he found a cute pink granite phone case and a book of 100+ recipes of cakes you can make in a coffee mug. He put that and some face masks and candy in a basket for Arriana to thank her for everything she's done for us.

Physics has been boring as hell, but it got easier when Zayne finally shook his cold. I was lucky I didn't catch it. That would have raised suspicion seeing as no one else at school got sick.

I'm sitting waiting for him to come into class when my phone buzzes.

I'm gonna be late. Not feeling too hot, could be a bit so don't panic when I'm not there

I stare at my phone for a minute. He couldn't be getting sick again, could he? I type a reply as the bell rings.

You're always hot ;) Where are you?

Mr. Roe comes in and starts taking attendance, Zayne's name is high on the list given his last name starts with a D.

"Anyone seen Zayne today?" Mr. Roe looks at us all, especially me, over the top of his glasses.

"He probably had a fairy convention to go to," Conrad mutters to his friends, making them all snicker.

They shut down when Mr. Roe takes off his glasses and stares at them, clearly less than amused.

"I saw him in the halls, he's probably in the bathroom or something," I say with a shrug as Mr. Roe looks back at the paper, marking him tardy I assume.

My phone buzzes.

In the bathroom by the office, I'm fine really. Just out of it today, take notes for me

After half of class goes by and he's still not here, I text him to make sure he's not hurt. No response.

"Mr. Roe?" I watch him as he turns from the blackboard,

stunned that someone interrupted him. "Can I go to the bathroom?"

He nods his head to the door and I leave. Once out of sight of the door, I dart to the bathroom Zayne said he was in.

I go in and it's so quiet. I don't see anyone or any feet under the doors, but I see a backpack covered in pins for Linkin Park, Neon Trees, Disney and more just like Zayne's. I text him to see if the backpack buzzes. When it does I knock gently on the door.

"Zayne?" I whisper. "What's going on, are you ok?"

I hear some movement and see feet drop onto the floor, he unlocks the stall door and steps out with his bag.

"I'm fine." But he clearly isn't. He looks pale and sick, his hair is a mess and his hands quake. "I didn't sleep well, I must have fallen asleep in here."

"Zayne you can barely stand up, what's going on?"

"Nothing!" He snaps and smacks my hand away when I try to steady him.

He stumbles. I catch him and sit him down against the wall.

"Zayne, I won't ask again. What's going on? Don't make me call your mom."

"Just tired and hungry, I guess. I couldn't sleep and when I missed my alarm I skipped breakfast."

This is a lot more than one bad night's sleep and one missed meal, I'm sure of it. My mind goes back to that first night at his place, when his mom asked if he would eat some dinner.

"Zayne, are you eating? Did you have dinner last night or anything?"

"Yeah a little, I was busy with..." He gets tense and stops to think for a second. "With homework."

"Tell me the truth."

His eyes meet mine. The bags under his eyes are so deep it hurts to see. Looking at him now, I notice how weak and thin he's become.

"I didn't eat yesterday. I couldn't."

I crouch down in front of him, running my hand through my hair in exasperation. "What the fuck Zayne? When did you last eat?"

"Day before last, I think."

"Why aren't you eating? Zayne you look like shit, and this is just on the outside, what do you think this is doing to your insides?"

He smirks weakly. "Wouldn't you love to know about my insides?"

"Zayne!"

"Josh." He puts his hand on my cheek. "I'll be ok, I promise. I'll have a big lunch, ok? Maybe tonight we can go to the park and you can bring something to eat."

I take his hand and tug him into a hug, not squeezing too hard out of fear of breaking him.

"I swear to god if you don't eat tonight..."

He gently kisses my neck, sending chills up my spine. "I promise, you can kick my ass if I don't. Get back to class, I'll be there eventually."

He starts to stand, refusing my help. I walk out of the bathroom, giving one last glance to make sure he's got his balance, before I head back to class and keep taking notes.

I spend the day bouncing between texts from Zayne and Arriana. She and I make a plan, I'll ask mom to make me a lunch before school, Arri and I will split her lunch money and give the bagged lunch to Zayne. Hopefully it will encourage him to eat.

Walking to the cafeteria, I get another text from Arriana.

Is he ok? I haven't really seen him at all today.

Arriana has no idea how bad he looked earlier, and I'd prefer to keep it that way. It was painful to see him like that. I don't want to scare her, especially given how close they've gotten the past few weeks.

I don't reply, instead meeting her in line for the lunch counter. "Trust me Arri, it wasn't good. I think I'm going to sit with you today, let me know if you see him. I want to make sure he eats something."

Arriana nods as she grabs an extra sandwich and extra cookie. She is very aware of what she eats, and given that one of the sandwiches had tomatoes, I know that they aren't both for her.

"I'm gonna put some of mom's cobbler in a Tupperware tonight, bring it to him for me?"

"Of course, you'll fatten him up in no time."

Caira and Tempe wave her over to a table near the back corner, I follow close behind. She sits down next to Caira and Tempe pulls my arm down next to her.

"Hey Josh..." She twirls her messy platinum hair and runs her hand down my arm. Arriana looks ready to puke.

"Tempe." I carefully take her finger and place her hand on the table. "I mean this in the best way possible. Not happening. Not if my life depended on it."

Tempe giggles and licks her lips. She leans over to expose the part of her chest that's popping out of her sparkly, strappy crop top.

"Yeah right, all you guys play hard to get. It's so fun."

She gets up to get a drink, taking the time to bend over to get her wallet and putting her small ass in her even smaller shorts in my face.

She struts off and Arriana looks ready to die. "I guess she finally gave up on Conrad." I shudder as Caira smirks in her compact mirror at the two of us.

"She's taking a break. You, Conrad, and that fruit loop are pretty much the only ones in the school she has yet to nail. Besides freshman." Caira finishes with her mirror and slams it shut. "I almost think you two would be cute. Maybe you could get her to stop fucking everyone she meets, I think she even did the popcorn boy at the movie theater, the one with the juvie record."

I stop listening when I see Zayne come into the lunch room, still stumbling around. He gets in line and starts grabbing food, putting me at ease.

He gets dirty looks from other people in line but ignores them as he stacks food on his tray.

Out of nowhere, I see Tempe point Zayne out to Conrad and his friends. Conrad taps on his friend's shoulder and whispers something that makes them cackle and fist bump. His friend takes his tray and walks up to Zayne. My stomach sinks as he starts talking to Zayne. Not even five minutes into their "conversation" Zayne ditches his tray and storms out of the lunch room, attracting a lot of looks, laughs, and fingers pointing.

It takes so much restraint to not run after him. Tempe soon returns with a Diet Pepsi. I half-heartedly listen to the girls talk while I try to keep myself in my seat, debating if risking outing myself is worth it.

"What just happened?" Caira looks confused as Tempe tries to sit on my lap with a cheeky grin.

"Conrad's buddy Trevor just totally roasted the fruit loop. Trevor took his tray up to the fairy and said that he could take his tray because the sight of him made him lose his appetite and want to puke. Figures he would run off like a little bitch."

I wait a few minutes and listen to Caira and Tempe talk while Arriana slips the extra food into my backpack. I barely touch my own meal before claiming I'm full and leaving the lunch room to find Zayne. I find him in the bathroom again.

"Zayne? It's me." This bathroom is always empty, no one wants to be this close to the office. "Zayne, open up."

He steps out of the stall as he throws his backpack over his shoulder, nearly knocking himself back.

I draw him into a hug, petting the back of his hair. He squeezes me and starts to sob, quickly turning into that odd hiccup thing that people do when they get hysterical. I try to calm him, sitting him down and putting his head in my lap.

He grips me like he's hanging off a cliff and I'm the only thing keeping him from free falling. I pull out some water for him as he tries to control his breathing.

"Please drink this, it should still be cold." He takes it out of my hand. "It'll cool you off."

"I hate this place," he mutters as I rub his arm.

"I know, it took a lot to not punch that dick in the face right there. One of these days I'm gonna smash their cars, I swear."

Zayne takes a deep, shuddering breath and holds the water bottle close. "They're just like my dad."

I stop for a second, stunned. "What do you mean?"

"Ever since I came out, he hasn't been able to sit at the table with me for more than a couple minutes. He just gets up, leaves his plate and disappears into his room. He can't eat around me, and I hate it. I hate it so much."

He starts to bawl again. I think about his mom and all her attempts at offering him food, the way he stopped eating the cookies after seeing his dad.

"Is that why you haven't been eating? How long has this been going on?"

"Since seventh grade, so like six years. He doesn't think he can eat around me, just like them, I make people sick. I can't even look at food without getting disgusted with myself over it." He starts sobbing again. "I want to go home."

I pull out my phone and call his mom and explain what happened. She says she'll be there in twenty minutes. I don't tell her about him not eating, after Zayne begged me not to and promised he'd try to eat the sandwich I brought him.

I sit with him while he calms down, eats, and composes himself. He kills the sandwich, water, and the cookie in the blink of an eye. I know he must still be hungry given there wasn't much there to make up for two days of not really eating anything, but at least it was something. I watch him leave for the office as I dry his tears off my shirt and then head back to the lunch room.

I get there not long before the bell rings, barely having time to turn around and head to class. Arriana has already disappeared with her friends to get stuff from her locker. I text her about Zayne before I get to English, sitting down and resting my head.

I have to do something. I've never seen him hurt that much, and I never want to let him go through it ever again.

AVOIDANCE MANEUVER #37

I get home and see my mom making her awesome beef stew. After she goes to bed I'll have to snag some for Zayne.

Mom and I talk about her packing my lunches for school. I tell her I just don't want to stand in line for food when I could get her better food for free quicker. A little flattery never hurts. I smirk as she waves me off. A chuckle escapes me as I go to sit in my room, pull up a story on my I've been writing on my laptop and relax and try to take my mind off everything.

"Ariel?" I hear the door open and my dad's voice boom through the house, "Everyone? I'm home!"

Arriana jumps out of her room and tackles him in a hug, her red hair a streak as she runs past the kitchen. Quickly leaving my desk, I follow her.

He catches her, the same way he did when he would return from a trip when she was six. They've always been super close. She's always been his princess. He kisses her head and asks her about school.

I wait until they've calmed down to follow mom out of the kitchen. He sees me and lights up. The longer the trips the more he misses us.

"How're you doing champ?" he asks me. "Your mom said you've been doing really good on your school work and have actually been getting out of the house. It's good to know you're back to your old self."

"Thanks Dad. It's been good, but we definitely missed you. Careful Arriana, now that he's home, you have to share that cobbler!" I call down the hall with a snicker.

"Never!" she hollers back.

The three of us joke as my dad drags me into a hug. "I really did miss you, kiddo. Go do your homework, we can all talk and catch up at dinner."

I nod and walk off, looking back to see him draw my mom into a kiss. I've never doubted how much they love each other. I want what they have. Maybe now I can have it.

I start my homework when my phone starts vibrating. Zayne is calling.

I put in my earbuds and hit the *answer call* button. "Hey, how are you feeling?"

He sounds exhausted. "I'm ok, my mom is really worried. I heard her talking to my dad about what happened, she sounded like she was crying. I am so tired. I don't know if I have the energy to comfort her. I mostly wanted to call and apologize about today. You shouldn't have had to see that."

"Zayne, don't start. I would have been there no matter what. I wanted to be there for you, what they did was shit and you shouldn't go through that alone. If I let you go through that alone what am I?"

"Eye candy," I hear the smirk in his voice and stop writing to let out a deep cackle.

"Have you eaten?" I inquire.

He hesitates.

"Zayne?"

"Yeah, I ate. My mom made me a frozen pizza and got me settled before she left to get groceries. I ate a few slices before taking a nap. How was the rest of your day?"

"Long, I was really worried about you." I check the light under my door to make sure no one is out there listening to me. "You can't do that to yourself, Zayne. Babe, you have to eat, I'm serious."

"I know, and I will. I'll try to be better, I promise."

I hear heavy footsteps come down the hall. "I have to go. I'll text you soon, please eat some more. I'll be sure to come over tonight. Bye."

I hang up as my door opens and my dad steps in.

"How's it going, champ? Need any help?" He hangs in my doorway, still in his suit. He stands stiff, looking around my room as he gives a forced smile.

"Just Physics, I finished everything else in my study hall period. You ok, Dad? You seem off today." I put down my pencil and take out my earbud.

"It was just a long trip. It's hard to always be away from your kids and your mom. It's nice to finally see you all and I want to take it all in before I have to leave again." He comes over to pat my shoulder, flashing another forced smile, "Dinner's almost ready, why don't you finish up and come out to the living room? You and I could watch some TV and chat for a bit."

I nod, nervous about what *to* talk about. There's so much I'm hiding, I don't know what to tell him. I take my time doing my work while I try to figure out what to do with my dad.

As dad walks out, I check my phone and see a text from Zayne, it's a picture of him lounging in his PJ's on his bed with a big slice of pizza in his mouth. He's wearing a purple shirt with the Disney logo and grey sweatpants. They look too big on him. None of his clothes fit him right, and part of me wonders if it's to hide the weight loss.

I send him a text.

Tomorrow will be better. Finish eating and rest, I'll see you tonight.

I put down my phone and finish my assignment. Walking into the living room, I hear my dad yelling at the football ref on TV. I used to love watching football, but this past summer I've kind of gotten bored with it. Every game is pretty much the same.

Dad calls me over to watch the game with him, and given how long he's been gone, I humor him. I listen to him yell at the players and ref even though they can't hear him. I start dozing off on the couch. Dad takes my shoulder lightly to tell me dinner is ready, prompting me to get up and go sit at the counter with my family.

We have a table, but we never use it. For some reason, we all silently agree to use the counter. I get comfortable on my stool while watching my mom pour out the stew into bowls for everyone, pouring hers last.

I sit and make half-hearted conversation while listening to Arriana gush about the school year so far. My dad listens intently as she goes on about her classes and the boys she likes. I try to be interested, but I'm tired and worried about Zayne.

I eat and excuse myself, causing my parents to exchange a worried look when I tell them I want to go to bed.

"Do you want some more food before you go to bed? Maybe take some cobbler with you? It's strawberry."

I give her a stiff grin before heading for the bedroom. "Maybe later, Mom. I'll probably get up and get some in the middle of the night. I'm sorry, I just feel really tired." I look at my dad who watches me with concern. "It's really good to have you home dad. Maybe this weekend we can go out to lunch."

He nods as I walk out. I fall into bed the second I reach my room. I text Arriana before closing my eyes, trying to ignore how I already hear my parents talking. I also try to ignore that I hear my name in their conversation, instead I just focus on the message to Arri.

Put some stew and cobbler in Tupperware for me? If you could wake me when Mom and Dad are asleep so I could go see Zayne I'd appreciate it. Love you guys.

I fall asleep faster than I ever imagined possible. I still have on my jeans and socks but I don't really care, especially if I'm going out tonight. I think I hear my phone buzz a couple times but I ignore it and embrace the lure of exhaustion.

I wake up five hours later, disoriented, and lurch to my feet. I don't know if anyone is still awake. I grab my phone and see the time, it's after ten o'clock and I have five texts from Arriana and four from Zayne. Opening his first, I stretch and get ready to go.

Is everything ok? You hung up really fast.

Josh? Are you ok?

Did I do something wrong? Please answer me

Arriana told me you're napping before coming over, let me know when you wake up. I miss you.

I read through Arriana's texts. All of them are her telling me that there's food for Zayne, that he called her because he was worried, and that Mom and Dad are in bed. Those are from an hour ago, and I can hear my dad snoring.

I hear my door creak open as Arriana peeks her head in. I start to slip on my shoes as she gives me the food and I thank her for calming Zayne down. She also hands me one of her special yogurt and strawberry chocolate bars to give to Zayne.

Before climbing out my window, I give her a hug and gather the food in my backpack. I slide outside and run for my bike, texting Zayne that I'm on my way.

Pedaling fast and hard down the road, I feel my phone go off in my pocket, I take it out and see Zayne's caller ID.

"Hey, sorry I hung up so fast earlier, my dad came home and wanted to talk." I start panting when I stop at a crosswalk.

"How long until you get here?" His voice sounds low and desperate.

"Ten minutes if I book it. Are you ok?"

He doesn't say anything for a minute. "Yeah, I just miss you right now."

"Alright, I'll be there soon, Arriana and I have some stuff for you so hopefully it'll help."

"Ok, see you soon. Bye."

"Bye."

He hangs up the call and I start peddling again. I make it there in a little over eleven minutes and stomp up the stairs.

His mom greets me at the door and tells me Zayne has been in his room all day.

"Today was really rough on him," she whispers.

"I so badly wanted to do something I just didn't know what I could do that would actually help." I put my head down, ashamed I didn't do more.

"Josh, honey, none of this is your fault," she continues. "There's only so much you can do to help. You were there when he needed someone, you called me to get him out of that bad situation. It would have been much worse had you done nothing. He's just struggling right now, aside from asking for some food, he's been avoiding me and everything else all day. Except you, so why don't you get in there?"

I nod and put my hand comfortingly on her shoulder before I head for his room. Opening the door I see him facing the wall in his bed.

"Zayne? Babe, what's going on?"

He rolls over and I see just how bad he's doing. His eyes are red and puffy and he's quivering. I dart over and sit next to him.

"My dad is thinking about sending me to a camp."

"What?" I don't fully understand what he's talking about, if it's what I think it is I might just punch a wall.

"When my mom was gone, I went in their room to find batteries for my TV remote. My dad keeps them in his desk, so I opened his drawer and found a brochure for a conversion camp. Josh, I'm scared."

Zayne starts sobbing again.

I bring him close to me and kiss the top of his head. "No one is going to take you away. I won't let it happen."

He sits and wails in my lap, holding me tightly as the panic fills the air. I try to comfort him, but I don't really know how to. I didn't even know there were camps anywhere near here. I didn't even know they were still legal.

I sit with him until he calms down, not long after, he falls asleep in my lap. I don't want to let him go, instead, I just wrap my arm around him and cradle his head.

Conversion camps were some of the things I came across during my research after that party freshman year. Stories of survivors haunted me with thoughts of electroshock therapy, verbal abuse, the use of drugs, and more. The thought of

Zayne, or anyone else, in a place like that makes me sick.

I carefully turn him and lower him onto his pillow. I bring his blankets up to his chin and slowly back up to sit in his desk chair. I sit there for over an hour before his mom comes to check on us.

"Josh, is everything ok? How long has he been asleep?" She comes over and kneels next to him, brushing a few strands of his pink hair out of his face.

"I have no idea, it feels like forever. He's just in such a bad place right now, I feel like I just need to stay right here to be here for him as much as I can."

"What happened?"

I don't know if I should tell her Zayne's fear, if she doesn't already know then I don't think Zayne will get sent away. His father wouldn't be able to do that without telling her first, and if I tell his mom how will he react?

"He's just...getting worn down by it all. It's all this negativity and pressure pushing on him."

I watch her as she watches him. I wonder if my mom ever did something like that to me or Arriana.

"I should get home." I pull out the food I brought and offer it to her. She takes it. "These are for him, the chocolate is special from my sister. Make sure he eats it?"

She nods and I leave quietly. I cry the whole way home, all

the way until I fall asleep.

I can't lose him. I can't.

DARK SIDE

Zayne has been on edge for a month now, terrified his father will send him to a conversion camp. Knowing the closest one is in Dallas doesn't help. The distance almost scares him more than the camp. He hasn't been sleeping and he's been struggling to not cling to me in public. Both of us have been struggling with that.

While he's struggling with the fear of being sent away, he's been trying hard to eat more and has made a little bit of progress. Some days are harder than others, especially with Conrad around.

Conrad and his girlfriend broke up two weeks ago, giving Tempe the opportunity she wanted. It's because of this that I now spend every day at lunch with my sister wishing I could strangle him with his own ego.

Zayne usually sits in the bathroom by the office at lunch just to get away from everyone. We take advantage of no one going in there to have a little bit of time to ourselves in the chaos of our school.

Every night I'm at his house, comforting him and giving

him the sense of security he needs. His father is coming home later and later, and talks to him less and less.

This is the seventh night in a row I've snuck out to see him. I must be breaking some record. Deep down I'm nervous. Tonight his parents will be out until really late trying to get some private time, so it'll just be me and Zayne.

We've been texting most of the day, he doesn't seem to be doing well.

I could bring a movie and some food? My mom made truffles

I don't know Josh. Tonight I think I just want to enjoy us being alone, after everything the past couple months has dropped I think we need just one night

Conrad has been giving him a really hard time at school, especially in first period. It's hard to start every day being tormented, and it's hard to watch. He's upped his game in finding new ways to torture Zayne. Over the weekend, he had someone break into Zayne's locker and stuffed it full of tiny stress balls shaped like the shit and cupcake emojis. He's been tripping him on the way to his desk in Physics when Mr. Roe isn't looking. He jumped Zayne on his way home last week giving him a massive black eye.

Part of me is afraid Zayne won't be able to handle it much longer. At lunch I'm proven right.

Zayne has been trying to get lunch in line, he's been trying to eat three meals a day. The downside is that being in line makes him an easy target.

I'm sitting at a table with Arriana, Tempe, Caira, Conrad, and his friends, off in my little corner next to my sister writing in my journal trying to ignore them. Conrad whispers something to Tempe causing her to giggle obnoxiously and run her hands all over him. I debate whether or not I should puke as he scoots her off his lap, gets up, and marches over to Zayne.

The table we're at is close to the lunch line, so I hear everything.

Conrad puts his hand on Zayne's shoulder, as if they've been friends forever.

"You know Cupcake, I really just want to extend my condolences. I can't imagine what your parents are going through, being forced to deal with your perverted ass every single day. They must be so embarrassed, feeling responsible for your sickness."

Arriana grabs my hand and loses all color in her face. Even Caira is taken aback and looks disturbed.

All I see is the last wire in Zayne snap. Suddenly in front of everyone, Conrad is on the floor holding his nose. Before anyone can react, Zayne is on top of Conrad hitting him and swearing and screaming.

"Don't you *ever* talk about my parents like that!" His fist meets Conrad's cheek, "I have put up with you and your shit for four years! I am so fucking sick of it!"

Conrad tries to cover his face and get away but Zayne has absolutely snapped. A few other guys and I jump up to break up the fight. One other guy helps me grab Zayne and yank him back off Conrad who is bleeding profusely from his nose.

The football coach comes up and grabs Zayne, tugging him out of my grasp.

"You call me the sick one you fucking asshole?" Zayne screams at the top of his lungs. His face is bright red. "You're the one who can't survive one day without making someone's life a living hell! And for what? I've never done *anything* to you! I just want to be me but all you want is to make me hate myself! You're the sick one!"

He gets dragged out of the lunchroom as everyone crowds around the scene.

Conrad struggles to stand up, his shirt stained and hair tousled. "What a fucking freak show."

For the first time since I met Conrad, I see the whole school turn on him. Starting with my sister and Caira.

"You might have taken it too far Conrad," Caira gives him

a disgusted glare. "Yeah he's weird and gross but what you said was bullshit that no one deserves."

Arriana actually *spits at him*! Conrad flinches, gawking at her with wide eyes and his mouth hanging open in shock.

"I hope you're happy," she barks, causing him to flinch again. "You have successfully destroyed him. And for what? Because he's different? Because you could? Because he *dared* to be himself? He's right, *you* are the sick one."

People mutter commentary, some siding with Zayne, some with Conrad, some even go as far to say they should both be expelled.

I take my chance in the midst of the chaos to run after Zayne and to try and defend him to the school. People like Conrad have gotten away with this shit for far too long.

I spend an hour in the office with a bunch of other kids picked at random to find out what really happened. I sit down with the counselor who writes down everything I say as I describe everything that Zayne said, and all Conrad has done since freshman year.

As I leave the office, I see Zayne in the principal's office, his head in his hands sobbing as our principal, Ms. Jennings, gently rubs his back and keeps talking to him.

Tonight is going to be really rough.

I spend every second of class watching my phone hoping to hear from Zayne. Silence.

I check when I get home. Nothing.

When my parents go to bed. Not a single text.

I call his mom. "Mrs. Daveen? It's Josh, is Zayne ok? I haven't heard anything, and I'm really worried. I don't know if I can still come over, but I at least want to make sure he's ok."

Her voice is stressed and sad.

"It's not looking good Josh. The school isn't sure what to do. No one ever actually reported this Conrad for what he did and while Zayne has been bullied nonstop, he *did* attack someone. *I* don't even really know what happened, he won't talk to us. I'm still going out with his father tonight, he's steaming over this whole thing. If you want to come over you can, I think you're the only one he'll talk to right now."

I slide out my window and take off on my bike minutes after I hang up. I'm over there just as his parents start to get into their station wagon.

His mom hugs me. "Thank you Josh, he needs someone right now. I'm afraid that if we push, we'll drive him farther away. We don't even know how the fight started."

His father stands there, firm and stoic as I tell them what happened and what Conrad said. His mom covers her mouth as tears start falling, his father closes his eyes and drops his head.

"Tiffany, get in the car," his voice booms over us. "I need a minute."

She nods, climbing in while wiping away tears. Mr. Daveen walks around the car and stands in front of me, towering over me. I try to stand my ground.

"I haven't taken the time to meet you." He glares down at me skeptically.

"I'm Josh, it's nice to finally meet you. Zayne will never admit it, but he really values your opinion and looks up to you."

Nothing on his face changes.

"Do you care about my son?"

"Yes, sir."

"Do you truly care? Or is this some sick joke like the crap pulled today?" His voice gets heavier and louder.

"With all due respect sir," I take a step closer. "I'm the one who's been making sure your son eats because he's been too disgusted by himself to do so since you can't seem to eat dinner with him."

"Now you listen he -"

"I've been here holding him while he cries in fear of you sending him to a conversion camp. I've held him until he's finally calm enough to sleep after the torture he endures every day at school. I've always respected his wishes even when it kills me, like when he begs me to hide our relationship for the sake of my sister and I's reputations. I care about your son more than he thinks you do."

He tightens his jaw. "I would *never* send my son to a group like that! I didn't know what they really were, as soon as I found out, I shredded that paper. I love my son, and I would *never* willingly be the reason he hurts himself. If you care about him as much as I do, as much as his mother does, as much as I hope you do, you'll get your ass in there and help him. You'll stand for him, and you'll protect him with all you have."

"Sir," I finally meet his eyes. They look so hurt as tears threaten to spill from them. "If I could I would never leave his side."

He reaches out his hand and shakes mine, his eyes still like daggers as he glares at me, before he gets in the car with his wife. I stomp up the stairs, looking back to see them both wailing, holding each other.

I so badly want them to heal.

I knock on the door, quickly greeted by a hellish looking Zayne. His shirt hangs off him, clearly about ten sizes too big, his entire body limply getting dragged along as he jerks me inside.

I don't get a single word out as he pushes me against the now closed door and slams his lips on mine. He holds the sides of my face and I can feel the heat radiating off of him.

I hold his waist tightly as he starts biting my lip and breathing heavily. I so badly want to talk to him and find out what happened, but part of me wants this to go on.

He moves his hands into my hair, now longer than when we first kissed, and starts grabbing it. He pulls back to grab my hand and drag me into his room.

Zayne won't meet my eyes as he pushes me back onto his bed and angles himself above me. He starts biting and kissing my neck.

"Zayne," I murmur. His hand goes up my shirt. "Zayne calm down. What's going on?"

He doesn't seem to be listening, his breath is hot and heavy on my skin. He yanks his shirt off, revealing the many bruises in different stages of healing. He starts to kiss me again, but I press my hands on his chest.

"Zayne! Please talk to me." His eyes are shining with tears. "Please."

"Josh..."He falls back and sits facing away from me at the foot of his bed, "I'm sorry. But please, for once don't ask questions, don't try and fix things, he went too far today. I couldn't take it anymore."

I prop myself up and sit behind him. I carefully place my hands on the sides of his arm, placing a soft trail of kisses on his shoulder.

"You shouldn't have to go through any of this, Zayne. If I could make it stop, I would. I would happily announce to the world that we're together if it would take the heat off you, I don't care anymore. I don't care what they do or say to me, neither does Arri. I want to be there for you, I want the world to know I'm here for you and care about you."

He jumps up and turns to face me. "No! You're not telling anyone, I'm not letting you go through any of this for me. You and Arriana don't deserve the shit I go through!"

"Zayne..."

"No! Now please just shut up for one night!" He comes over and tugs my shirt over my head as he starts to kiss me again, his hand cupping my cheek.

I reach up to grab his wrist to bring him back. His skin feels rougher than I remember, he starts trying to tug his hand away.

I jerk away from his kiss and look at his wrist. It's covered in deep red cuts. He still fights to get his arm away from me.

"What the hell is this?" I yell at him as he finally pulls away.

He doesn't say anything. He stands a few steps away and I don't think I've ever seen him so damaged. His shoulders are slumped and he's covered in bruises, I'm now seeing a small amount of blood smearing on the inside of his wrists.

I come up and grab both his arms, facing his wrists to the ceiling. They're both incredibly cut up.

"Zayne. Why would you do this?"

"What else can I do? Nothing's going to change, and I'm so sick of bottling up how much it hurts. I hate how much it hurts and how often I feel what they say is right, at least this way the pain is real!"

"Zayne! Stop!" I hold his shoulders. "None of what they say is true! There is *nothing* wrong with you! Your pain is valid, even if it shouldn't even be here, it is valid."

I press him close to me and hug him. He and I drop to our knees as he tightly holds me, burying his face into my shoulder.

I get him into bed and hold him in my arms until his parents come home. By then he's calmed down and fallen asleep.

I sit with his parents and explain everything that happened and everything he's going through. You can see in their faces they think they've failed. I tell them that none of it is their fault.

"I think I might have something to help," I finally say. They look at me, confused and hopeful. "I need your permission to take Zayne for the day on Saturday."

ACCEPTANCE

Zayne isn't at school the next day. He technically isn't suspended because the school is afraid of a lawsuit, but the principal and his parents agreed he needs a few days away from the people at school

I walk into Physics and am shocked to see Conrad and his bandaged nose sitting in his seat.

"What are you doing here?" I ask, fighting the urge to hit him.

"Well, most teenagers come to school five days a week in an effort to learn, so I thought I'd take part." he gives me a smirk.

"You treat someone like shit everyday for four years and you still aren't even suspended? You still dare show your face after the well deserved ass kicking you got?"

He gets up and gets in my face. I hold my ground. "You got a problem with me, Notes?"

I drop my bag and slam my book on the desk, finally over it all. "You know what Conrad? I do, I really do. Zayne did nothing to aggravate you. He did nothing to deserve your shit, but you still made his life a living hell. I do have a problem with you!"

"What do you care about that freak? He brought this on himself when he decided to be a disgusting pervert!"

I grab his shirt and twist. "Don't call him that! He's twice the man you are!"

Conrad looks scared for a second, but once the flip switches in his head, I know I've fucked up. "Wait a second..." He chuckles. "Are you...and Cupcake...No way."

His voice is low as I stare at him, seeing red.

"Conrad I will say this once," I say in a low voice. "If you treat Zayne or *anyone* like that ever again I will kick your ass so hard you'll need a hospital. I've seen you walk the halls like you own them for far too long. Your reign is over."

His eyes get dark and I feel him shudder a little as I drop him and gather my shit to head to my seat, ignoring the stares and whispers from the students around us, some stepping away from me or avoiding eye contact. I look up and see Mr. Roe watching from outside the classroom. He comes in and acts like nothing happened.

He starts teaching and I just stare out the window. Today is Friday. Tomorrow is Saturday. Today needs to end faster.

Conrad looks back at me halfway through class. I elect to

pretend I don't notice. I know it's a very real possibility I might get outed before lunch. At this point though, I don't think I care.

The day drags on, and Conrad keeps his mouth shut for all of it. Now he's the one alone at lunch. Even Tempe ditched him. It feels good seeing him get a taste of his own medicine.

I dart through the day so I can get home and prepare for tomorrow. I don't care about any classes or even how my English teacher tries to convince me to enter a writing contest, my mind is too consumed with tomorrow. I brief Arriana on what's happening and ask her to cover. She agrees and says she'll tell mom and dad that I'm with her and Tempe. Tempe has moved on from Conrad back to me, so we're certain she'll tell people she was with me if she's asked.

I spend an hour on the phone with Zayne telling him to be ready by 10:00 tomorrow morning, that we're borrowing his dad's car and going on a small trip. He begs to know what's going on but eventually gets tired and goes to bed.

By 10:30, I've followed his lead. I climb into bed, grabbing my game controller to pass time. I feel myself slowly dozing off, eventually laying down and praying my plan works. It has too.

I wake up to the sound of Arriana rummaging through my closet.

It's 8:00 AM. "Can I help you?"

She straightens up and turns, beaming with excitement, "I want to help you get ready! I'm thinking the red dip dye shirt and your black jeans."

"Arriana, it's not a fashion show." I climb out of bed and she starts fussing with my hair.

"I know, but it is still really important. You should try to look nice, maybe shower." She cringes at my messy hair.

I smirk and push her hand away before laying back down. I fall asleep again easily enough even with her babbling about my clothes.

I wake up again an hour later and finally drag myself out of bed. I can hear Arriana in her room next to mine. Our rooms share a bathroom, so every time she does any part of her thirty-part morning routine, I hear it. It's part of why I wake up later. I just shower and I'm done. I don't want to wait and listen to her for an hour.

I see she had a field day with my closet, as now all my clothes are folded, on hangers, and organized. I actually don't mind.

Hopping in the shower, I can't stop chuckling and trembling. Today is really important, it could be a really big stepping stone for Zayne and helping to accept himself and let go of all the pain he's holding.

I step out of the shower to grab my jeans and find my sister on my bed.

"Holy shit!" I put my hand over my heart to keep it in my chest after her sudden appearance, "Ever heard of knocking? You're lucky I'm wearing a towel."

She smiles wide. "Zayne called, he's ready whenever you want to go get him. I emptied your backpack and filled it with snacks since you guys will probably be gone all day. Get dressed! You gotta get going!"

"Arri, we don't need to be there until 11:00. If he and I leave in half an hour we'll still get there with time to get breakfast."

I grab my clothes off the chair by my closet before locking myself in the bathroom again. I toss the clothes on and come out to grab my shoes.

"Are you ready?" Arriana asks.

"I'm so much more than ready. So much is riding on today."

I slip on my shoes and grab my bag, running down the hall to meet Arriana in the yard. I give my mom a kiss and wait for her to go inside before mounting my bike and leaving.

I make it to his house by 9:20. His parents are already there with Zayne and the car keys.

Mrs. Daveen is talking to Zayne in the car. I lock my bike on the stairs before I stride over to see them.

"You scratch my car and I'll beat you," Mr. Daveen says gruffly. "Here's $50. Make sure he eats and call us when you're on the way back. We'll wait up for you."

I nod, taking the money and the keys, and thank him. I make my way to the car and say a quick hello to Mrs. Daveen. She looks as excited as I feel. I get in the driver's seat next to Zayne, who needless to say, looks tired and irritated.

"Where are we going?" He has a blanket in his lap and he gives me a frumpy pout.

"It's a surprise." I turn the engine over, driving off with a wave to his parents.

"Is this the part where you kill me and ransom my corpse to my family?"

"Zayne what the hell?" I start snickering, only slightly disturbed.

"Murder shows, I couldn't sleep." He tugs the blanket up past his shoulders. "My parents were up last night talking about what happened at school. I guess the principal wants to help us fight what happened these past few years, but my parents are wondering if it will do more harm than good. Like, why poke the sleeping bear?"

"Zayne, babe, I hate to break it to you but you and Conrad already kind of poked the bear a bit."

He puts his forehead on the window. The past two days have been really hard, not just on him. At school people are talking about Zayne, rumors are spreading that he got expelled or he *did* get sent away to a camp. Zayne's just sat in his room in bed. He's been so quiet. His mom and dad have been alternating staying home with him. Finding out he hurt himself really took a toll on all of us.

"Why don't you try and rest some? We're going to be driving for close to two hours," I reach over and place my hand on his knee, giving him a gentle squeeze, "It'll be ok."

He closes his eyes and I slip out a CD I made a couple weeks ago with all of Zayne's favorite songs including Everybody Talks by Neon Trees and some Linkin Park songs. The first song to play is Heavy, by Linkin Park and Kiiara.

About halfway through the song, Zayne starts muttering in a sleepy, low voice. "Words can't express just how heavy everything *really* is."

My heart aches hearing how hopeless his voice is becoming. We keep driving and soon the gentle motion puts Zayne to sleep. I take a granola bar from my bag and try to drive just a little faster.

It takes a little less than an hour and a half before we hit

Dallas. As we approach the community center I start to gently urge Zayne to wake up.

"Are you hungry?" I ask as he straightens up and stretches.

"Kind of," He looks around and tries to wake up, "Where are we?"

"Dallas, how do waffles sound?" I see a Waffle House close by and head in that direction when he starts nodding.

I let him pig out. I've saved every penny from my job since his birthday is coming up in three weeks, but I think letting him splurge will really help his current state.

We kill time with hot chocolate and small talk until a quarter to eleven. At that point I drag him away from his sugar and head down the street to the community center. I take his hand and walk inside. The first thing we see is a sign reading:

"Love Yourself Support Group for LGBTQ+ 11 AM-1 PM".

"Josh, what is this?" Zayne looks nervous.

"I found this group a month ago, I was planning to come after graduating. I think it could help. Will you try it?"

He wraps his arms around himself and bites his lip, "You'll stay with me?"

I nod and we walk in together along with around twenty other people, all of us taking a seat in a circle of fold out chairs.

Everyone mingles while I try to calm Zayne down. I slide my chair closer and hold his hand as a tall woman in a T-Shirt and jeans comes to join us in the circle.

"Welcome to the Love Yourself Support Group. This is a safe place to discuss and share your stories and receive support and resources. If you choose to share, please tell us your name, sexuality, and/or gender identity. My name is Marissa, I'm bisexual and have been head of our outreach program for six years now."

She tells her story of getting caught with a classmate and kicked out of her house at sixteen and how she almost OD'd on the street before finally coming to accept herself. When she's done another person raises their hand.

"My name is Devin, I'm non-binary and I came out two years ago. My family supported me as best they could but they didn't know what it meant to be non-binary, and at school and in town I wasn't met with much kindness. Kids would yell at me and tell me I was stupid, older people would try to scold me and say 'there's only two genders'.

"For a while I was confused and thought maybe I was gender-fluid, but I didn't really feel male *or* female. Last year I came into my school to find everyone had shoved bible verses and conversion camp pamphlets in my locker. I felt really isolated and even tried to kill myself. My parents have since put me into therapy where I was referred here. I know I shouldn't have tried to kill myself but at times it is really hard to deal with the cruelty I face regularly."

Marissa turns to face Devin and expresses that we live in a world still struggling to accept the LGBT+ community and that many people will have hurtful things to say. She expresses that in reality, these people and their opinions have no power over how we love and identify.

A few more people share, including a gender-fluid person who was attacked in a library bathroom because they chose to use the bathroom they identified with instead of "what was in their pants." Zayne squeezes my hand throughout all the stories; during the short break I encourage him to share. He hesitates and asks for some space.

I go talk to Marissa, explaining why we're here and what I hope to accomplish. She recommends I share in an effort to make Zayne feel secure. After we all sit she looks to me and I nod.

"My name is Josh, I'm gay and still haven't come out to anyone but my sister and obviously, my boyfriend." I look at Zayne and meet his shocked gaze with a careful smile. "I've been afraid to come out because of how people treat us where I live, but seeing how awful they treat someone I really care about... Someone I think I love, it makes me want to scream from the rooftops just so maybe I can finally defend him and take some of the pressure away."

Zayne looks speechless.

When asked why I haven't come out and revealed my relationship, I talk about my family and how Zayne doesn't want to put me in that position. I stop sharing but my mind doesn't stop going. I see Zayne slowly sit up and lean forward in his seat. He raises his hand and waits for Marissa to acknowledge him.

"My name is Zayne." His voice wavers a bit. "I'm gay and came out in seventh grade..."

He tells the group everything he's been through, even his eating disorder and his recent fight with Conrad. When he starts talking about his dad or what Conrad said, he starts looking ready to burst into tears. I reach out for his hand and hold it tightly. He's met with all types of support from group members, all telling him that none of what they say is valid and that they're just ignorant.

Marissa tells him to focus on the good, to focus on those in his corner rather than those against him; she looks at me as she speaks. He starts tearing up a little as she provides kind words of encouragement and commends him on his strength through the years.

After the group disbands, a lot of people come up to us and tell us they are proud of how strong we are and offer Zayne hugs and words of understanding and validation. Devin came up and talked to Zayne, saying how they wish they could stand up to their tormentors. A lot of people say the same, and tell him that he's not alone. He and I exchange phone numbers with some of the group while we keep talking about how best to handle the hate, walking away and when to get others involved.

The car ride home, Zayne just watches out the window. I don't know what he's thinking but don't ask. He's had a long day and I think he needs to just clear his mind.

I take him home and put him to bed. I fill in his parents and head to the mall where I meet Arriana. I text Zayne telling him to call me whenever he feels ready and go enjoy some time with my sister.

Monday is going to be special. Everything is going to change.

The Last Straw

I don't hear from Zayne until late Sunday. He says talking about everything made it all seem real and that finally acknowledging the pain took some of it away. He talked to his mom and dad on Saturday to clear the air. I am invited over Sunday night and arrive to see him and his dad at the table, eating together, cackling at something on TV.

After he and his dad finish up, Zayne hauls me into his room with a big grin. It seems he is slowly putting some of the pieces back together.

I stay most of the night. We talk, we kiss, and he finally keeps his promise to play the violin for me. He plays an instrumental version of Be Alright by Dean Lewis. I don't think I've heard anything so beautiful. The look on his face is a look of release. I can see how safe he feels, how free from reality he is when he plays. I sit on the edge of his bed, watching in awe.

I beg him to play more, but he insists on putting the violin up for the night.

"You know, I wanted to call you after you dropped me

off," Zayne says, sitting down next to me on the bed. "That group was really...I don't even know. I hate how many people go through this, but knowing I'm not alone takes so much pressure away. And when you shared, I...did you mean everything you said?"

I look at him and grin deviously as I entice him into a kiss. "Every single word," I whisper against his lips.

"Can I tell you something?" He presses his forehead to mine. "I think I love you too."

I draw him close to me and hold on tight. He holds me so tight that he has my shirt bunched up in his fists.

"I can't keep watching you go through everything alone. I can't just sit and do nothing," I breathe in his ear.

Zayne stays silent and holds me tighter. When he finally leans back it's to kiss me.

There is a knock at his door and we break apart. Zayne jumps up to answer the door. It's his dad.

"It's getting late, you two," Mr. Daveen says. "You should probably think of going home, Josh, and Zayne you need to go to bed. You're going back to school tomorrow and I want you both rested in case anything happens. We talked to the principal and she will personally keep an eye on things. If someone even looks at you funny, Zayne, tell her."

Zayne nods as I get up and put my arm around his shoulders. "It'll be ok, you won't be alone. I promise." I kiss him on the cheek and slip past his dad.

I look back from the front door and watch Zayne's dad hug him and tell him he'll always support him. He tells Zayne to be strong and that he can always talk about what's going on. He tells him he always has someone in his corner, I hope my parents will offer the same support and I can't help but envy the support system he has.

Everyone is asleep when I get home. Arriana is passed out at her desk, so I drape a blanket over her and slide a pillow in place of her notebook. I can hear my dad snoring. It's just me.

I go to my room and slip out of my jeans and shirt, replacing them with a comfy pair of sweats as I climb in bed with my phone.

I love you Zayne. Sleep well, I'll see you tomorrow <3

I plug everything in and turn off my light. Tomorrow is going to be heavy, between the rumors, Conrad, and the fact that I will *not* just stand by and watch Zayne suffer anymore.

Closing my eyes I hear Zayne's voice in my head.

"I think I love you too."

I fall asleep and before I know it, it's morning. My alarm hasn't gone off, but still I get up and go to see if Arriana is awake. She is.

"Hey," I whisper, opening her door a crack. "Can I come in?"

She looks up and brushes her hair out of her face. "Yeah what's up? How's Zayne?"

I grin. "He's good. Things are...really good, actually."

Her eyes get wide. "What happened? Why do you look like a fourteen year old at a Justin Bieber concert?"

"I told him I love him, and he told me he loves me too."

I chuckle as she jumps in her chair and comes to hug me.

She sits down with me on her bed and asks for the details. I tell her all about the group and Zayne with his violin and him asking if I meant what I said. We sit there for almost an hour.

"I don't even care that we're in high school and the odds are so stacked against us lasting as a couple. It feels so real." She squeezes my hand as I speak. "Arriana, I don't want to hide it anymore. I can't just sit back and pretend I don't care when people attack him, I can't."

"And you shouldn't. Plus you suck at faking it." She giggles at her little comment as I take a firm hold of her hands.

"What about you? I don't want this to affect you."

Arriana answers with a strong punch to the shoulder.

"Shut up! Nothing anyone can say or do will change that you deserve to be happy, you know I won't hesitate to put someone in their place. I just want you to be happy Josh, and I know Zayne is what makes you happy. You should own it!"

I thank her profusely before she goes to get ready for the day.

I have enough butterflies in my stomach to make a doctor faint. I so badly want to find Zayne as soon as I get to school and hit the "fuck it" button. I want to be there for him without having to hide.

I go back to my room and put my stuff in my bag. As soon as Arriana is done in the bathroom, I jump in the shower, eager to get to school. As a senior in high school, the thought of school should make me want to die, but I honestly can't wait.

When I get out of the shower I hear my phone ring. It's Zayne's mom.

"Mrs. Daveen? Is everything ok?" It's not normal for her to call me, let alone this early in the morning.

"Zayne's already left for school, he didn't have to leave for another twenty minutes but he did. I would appreciate it if you could get there soon to make sure he's ok. If anything happens please call me."

"Of course, I'll leave as soon as I can. I won't let anything happen today."

I hang up and grab some clothes to throw on. As I do my alarm goes off and I smack the off button. I shove my phone, laptop, and journal in my backpack before stumbling down the hall.

Arriana comes out of her room, concerned. I tell her Zayne is already at school alone and I need to be there in case someone tries anything. She grabs her bag and rushes after me while putting on her Lita heels. We're surprised to find Mom already in the kitchen with breakfast.

"Mom?" Arriana jumps. "What are you doing out here already?"

"Your dad had an early meeting I helped him get ready for, thought I'd get an early start on breakfast. I made your favorite breakfast sandwiches."

She hands us our breakfast sandwiches in bags and comes to give us both a kiss. I take it in as much as I can. I know today might really change how she sees me.

I get on my bike and take off for school as Arriana calls Caira to tell her that she's ready to go whenever. I get there in less than ten minutes and rush inside. Plenty of students have shown up, mostly freshmen who come in to study in the library.

I see Zayne standing alone at his locker, sorting his stuff. I let out a sigh of relief and bring my phone out to tell Arriana everything is ok so far. I go to my locker and open it to sort my stuff when the front door opens and more of my classmates start flooding in.

As they all look and see Zayne, most freeze, others start muttering under their breaths asking why he's here. He hears them but chooses to ignore them.

I send him a text as fast as my fingers will let me.

Remember how many people you have in your corner. They have no power, we're all here for you

He sees the text and looks up, making eye contact with me, and lights up. He gives a slight nod before shutting his locker and leaning back on it.

His excitement fades as quickly as it appeared. When I look around to see what he's looking at I see Conrad, his nose still bruised. He sees Zayne and I swear his ears start smoking.

He marches over to Zayne. "What the hell are you doing back? Shouldn't you be in some pervert camp? After what you did to me, you're lucky you weren't arrested!"

"Conrad, I'm not doing this," Zayne replies calmly. "I'm not going to put on a show for you to let you look tough and cool, I'm done letting you dictate my life." Zayne shrugs past him and heads in my direction.

Conrad does not react well.

He grabs Zayne's arm and shoves him back into the lockers, hard enough that Zayne's head whips back into the metal doors.

"You fucking faggot! You think I need *you* to look tough? You're so pathetic and I swear I'll make you pay for that little stunt of your last week! You'll wish you could crawl back home and die!" He grabs Zayne's shirt and slams him into the lockers again.

Hell no.

I drop my bag and run over, shoving Conrad so hard he crashes to the floor. Zayne drops and I carefully help him up.

"Josh!" I look back and see Arriana, she looks confused and scared.

"Get Mrs. Jennings!" I yell back and she takes off down the hall. I look back at Conrad. "I warned you to back off. I'll say it one last time because I don't want to hurt you, stay away Conrad."

He gets up fuming mad. He lunges at me, landing his fist on my cheek and knocking me down.

"Admit it, Notes, I knew the second you confronted me last week so just admit it!" I get up as Conrad yells. He tries to punch me again but I jump away. "You're a pervert just like Cupcake here! You both are vile abominations. I hope you two burn in hell together! You act like high and mighty, but in the end, you're just a couple of faggots who mean nothing!"

I punch Conrad in the stomach and he keels over. Half the school is watching as I stumble and catch my breath. I've never been a violent guy, but Conrad has taken it too far, and he needs to be taken down a few pegs. Conrad lays in the fetal position at my feet as I walk over to Zayne.

"Are you ok?" I ask quietly as I place my hands on his shoulder. "Zayne?"

"Josh what did you do?"

He looks terrified as I grab him, drawing him into a tight hug. "I don't care. I'm not hiding anymore, I'm not letting it happen."

Soon, Arriana and Mrs. Jennings arrive. I explain what happens and she asks a few others, including Caira, if that's really what down. Everyone, surprisingly, tells her we're telling the truth. She has the P.E. teachers escort Conrad to the nurse's office while she calls Zaye and me into hers.

We make it clear that Zayne tried to avoid conflict and that Conrad was the first to attack. She sits us down by her office with some other kids.

I look up and see Arriana in the office doorway. She looks devastated. I stand up, already wondering if I've fucked things up for her. "Arri?"

She looks at me and Zayne before bringing her bag closer to her.

"Caira called you both freaks and yelled at me," she says quietly. "She said that if I knew this the whole time it makes me just as disgusting and I must be a perv too."

"Arriana." My shoulders slump. "I'm so sorry."

"If she really feels that way then you know what? Screw her." She looks down. "It just hurts to hear such hateful words after all the years of friendship. Are you two ok?"

I look over at Zayne, who looks ready to break down. I sit next to him and take his hand.

"I did what they said," Zayne whispers. "I didn't let him get to me, I didn't let him get what he wanted. He should have walked away, why didn't he?" He sounds hysterical.

"Zayne--"

"No! You and Arriana shouldn't have to deal with this shit. He should have walked away! You shouldn't have got involved, Josh! You shouldn't have to deal with any of this! You shouldn't have to deal with me and my crap!"

He shoves me away as he gets up and runs out of the office. I go to chase after him but he's too fast. I come back to the office, shaking my head when Arriana gives me a hopeful look. I watch her face darken as any trace of joy or hope or excitement disappears.

Next thing I know, Mr. and Mrs. Daveen are at the school demanding to know what happened and saying Zayne isn't at home. Then my parents show up.

They ask all the same questions as Zayne's parents, wanting to know what happened and why I got punched, why Arriana was bawling her eyes out.

Things are not looking good for any of us. I sit there texting Zayne with no responses, his mom watches me hoping for something.

Nothing.

I get sick of it, sick of the questions and yelling. I get up and take off to find Zayne, leaving everyone at the school confused and scared.

Dark Thoughts And Dim Lights

I run to the park, hoping he's there since his parents said he wasn't home, but it's full of kids. I run to his apartment complex and search the parking area, the pool. Nothing. I run up the stairs to his apartment and start banging on the door.

"Zayne! Zayne are you in there?"

No answer.

"Zayne come on. Your parents are worried about you. I'm worried about you. Arriana is worried about you. Arriana knew I wasn't going to hide anymore. She doesn't care what people say, she cares about me. She cares about you, about us."

Whipping out my phone, I call Zayne's mom. She tells me where to find the spare key to get inside. She also knows they didn't lock the door. I dig for the key, finding it under the planter by their door, and shove it in the lock. I run inside and trip over something. It's completely dark in here. All the blinds are closed and the lights are out.

"Zayne?" I let out a harsh whisper, "Come on where are you?"

I take out my phone, turning on the flashlight. The

apartment is, for the most part, clean and tidy, but a couple chairs are knocked over and Zayne's backpack is on the floor by the coffee table.

His door is closed. The lights are out in there too. I don't see or hear anything. The entire apartment is still. I'm almost afraid that I'm walking into some horror movie shit.

I go into his room and find the light switch, illuminating the room and finding him curled into a ball on his bed.

I sit next to him. "Zayne?"

He's got himself buried in blankets, only the top of his pink hair poking out. He's vibrating, making the bed move with him.

I draw the blanket off his face to find him squeezing his eyes shut, whining to hold back sobs. I pet the back of his head slowly.

"Zayne, you scared us. Arriana and your mom sat in the office staring at me hoping that you would respond to my texts."

He starts sobbing, pressing the blanket to his eyes. "Why did you do that?" he asks between the hiccups.

"Do what?" I run my hand down his neck to his shoulder.

"Why did you come out like that? Why did you get in the middle of it? Why let yourself get outted? I never wanted anyone to say those things to you, or Arriana! I never wanted your parents to find out the way mine did, because of a fight!"

"I promise you, it's all ok. I was so sick of hiding it, hiding you, and Arriana and I knew what the backlash would be. We didn't care Zayne, living an ugly truth is better than a constant lie. Arriana encouraged me to do this. My parents though..." I take a minute and think of my journal, "Zayne, I couldn't even start to tell you how many times I've tried to figure out the perfect way to tell them, how many times I prepared a 'perfect' speech. I'd rather they find out by me standing up for someone, and someone I care about, instead of me telling them in a pre-planned conversation. I'm happy to finally be free of a lie, I'm happy I can really be here for you now, the only thing I'm not happy about is how you're feeling right now. None of this is your fault, Zayne. Conrad brought this whole thing down on us, he's the one who made it messy."

Zayne just lays there, jerking in place. I try to peel his blankets back but he fights me to keep them close. I grab tightly and pull as hard as I can, revealing him shirtless with deeper cuts now on his arms and even some blood soaked into the sheets.

My heart stops, most of the cuts aren't bleeding anymore but a few still are. I don't know what to say.

"Zayne..."

He grabs the blanket and tugs it back up to his chin. I get

up and leave the room, not taking my eyes off him as I call his mom.

"Can you or Mr. Daveen come get us? He's not doing good, he can't be alone right now. I need to talk to my parents and I know I have to face the consequences of the fight but I can't leave him."

She tells me she's on her way. Zayne's dad and my dad are both heated and yelling at the counselors and Mrs. Jennings.

I go back to sit with Zayne, getting him out a fresh shirt and his hoodie. He refuses to get up until his mom opens the door. He sits up and glances at her for a second before yanking the shirt from my hand. His eyes are dark and drooping. As he throws his shirt on his mom starts wailing at the sight of his arms.

Zayne pushes past her and walks out the door, leaving me to comfort her as she tries to hold back the tears.

"My baby," she sobs quietly, "They've destroyed him, they took his spirit and stomped it out, they've taken my baby from me."

She weeps into my shoulder for a minute before composing herself enough to drive.

Zayne wanted to sit alone in the back for the short ride. His mom and I keep glancing back at him. When we park back at the school I take Zayne to the nurse while Mrs. Daveen goes to continue with the principal.

The nurse cleans his cuts before putting gauze over them and wrapping his wrists tightly. She gives a sad, concerned look before he slips on his hoodie and walks out.

He doesn't look at anyone, not even me or even Arriana, as he sits in the corner bouncing his leg. He put his headphones in and I can hear his music from three seats over.

"Josh..." Mrs. Jennings peaks around the corner of the doorway. "Your parents want to talk to you."

I feel sick to my stomach, giving my sister one last smile before taking my final walk. I walk to Mrs. Jennings's office where she leaves me and my parents to talk in private.

I sit across from them in the empty seat in front of Mrs. Jennings' desk.

"Josh..." My mom's voice is tender and calm. "What happened?"

"Conrad crossed the line one too many times, he shouldn't get away with--"

"That's not what I mean honey." She leans forward. "What happened? What made you think that you couldn't tell us?"

I look at my dad who is still red in the face.

"I was afraid to let you down, that you wouldn't be able to look at me the same. That you wouldn't look at me as your son anymore. I wanted to but I...I just never knew how and my fear always got the best of me. I didn't want to lose you guys."

A flip switches in my dad. He turns to face me, leans forward in his chair with his jaw clenched and his finger raised and pointed at me.

"Joshua." His eyes start to shine with tears. "Don't you *ever* think we'll stop seeing you as our son, or that we'll stop loving you! I still remember holding you for the first time when you were born. I made a promise that day, when I held all eight and a half pounds of you, that I would always love and support you when you needed it. Your mother and I could never be disappointed in you for being yourself."

"How long have you know you're gay?" my mom asks.

"Since the summer after freshman year. I told Arriana because I had to tell someone. I was just so scared you would shrug it off or try to change me because I was different."

My mom comes in and hugs me, "Honey there is nothing wrong with different. Different is what gives your sister the courage to stand up for people she's never even met. It's what gave you the strength to help put a stop to the way that boy was being treated." She looks at me and runs her hand over the top of my head. "I wish we could have known about him. I would have loved to meet him and talk. I'm assuming that's where a lot of my food and Tupperwares have gone."

We chuckle and I nod.

"He's had it really rough and I just, I want him to know he's not alone. That he has me regardless of what anyone thinks. He deserves so much better than he has."

I look out the window into the main office and see him slouched in his chair, half asleep.

My dad grabs mine and my mom's hands and squeezes.

"Maybe you could tell us about him?" he says, directing the question at me. "Heck, maybe this weekend, his family can come over for dinner."

I relax as my mom sits back in her chair. "How did you two meet?"

Talking about this takes a load of pressure off of me, and I already feel like a wall has come down between the three of us.

I tell them everything, from seeing him in the mall, to our first kiss, to the group session. They aren't happy I've been sneaking out, but they do say they understand why I thought I had to. I tell them about Zayne and his family, I talk about how beautiful it is to listen to him play the violin. I talk about all the nights I watched him cry, I tell them he's been really struggling mentally and self destructing and how much it kills me to see him fall apart. It reaches a point where I look out at Zayne and I break. Tears start running down my face uncontrollably.

My parents drag me into a hug.

"It's ok honey," my mom whispers repeatedly into my ear. "We're all in this together now. We'll find a way to make it better."

We talk some more and then finally give Mrs. Jennings her office back. She suspends Conrad for a week starting next week and tells his parents there is a real chance for expulsion as he has now received a warning but continues harassing students.

Zayne is offered another week to stay home, with me bringing him his homework so he doesn't fall behind.

I talk to his parents, trying to figure out where we go from here.

"He said he really doesn't want to go to therapy, but we need to consider it at this point," Mr. Daveen tells us in a low voice. "If he isn't improving within two weeks I really think one on one therapy is what he needs. We're going to search high and low for a therapist that will treat him right and make him feel safe. He's been terrorized enough."

"I really want Zayne to meet my parents. We'd love you guys to come over on Saturday for dinner. I don't know, maybe it will help," I shrug and shove my hands in pockets, suddenly nervously excited at where things are heading, "I hope seeing all the support we have will help cheer him up a little. Plus my family really wants to get to know all of you, especially him."

They light up and say thank you before going to set up the details with my parents. I look and see Zayne glance over at how everyone is communicating. Arriana and my parents are openly talking and joking with his parents, so I go sit next to him.

He takes out an earbud.

"I'm sorry Josh." His lip quivers, "I didn't mean to let you down or upset anyone. I just couldn't handle it. I did what they said in the group and it didn't help. Hearing Conrad talk about you like that, hearing people talk down to Arriana. I felt like it was all my fault and I couldn't handle putting you through any of that."

I tug him into a quick kiss before looking him in the eyes.

"What people say or do is on them. Nothing anyone says about us will change how I feel, nothing they say is your fault, and nothing they can do will make any of us disappointed in you. Things should start looking up now. Conrad is getting suspended. You'll be free of him for two weeks. Plus, this Saturday, you're all coming over to *my* house."

He looks up in surprise and tentatively matches my smile. I take his hand and walk him to the door where his parents are waiting. They take him into a loving embrace as they walk off and drive home.

I turn to my family and go to join them, meeting my own

loving circle of embrace.

"I love you guys," I whisper to them all.

We leave to go home too. Arriana and I have been sent home to recover from the intense day. I have a feeling there will be a lot of recovering together as a family tonight.

Welcomed Healing

I've stopped sneaking out at night and hiding my texts. All week, everyday after school I go over to Zayne's house to bring him homework and notes. I end up staying for an hour or two helping him figure everything out before I go home.

Arriana and I have had it a little rough this week. We definitely get dirty looks now that I'm out of the closet, but with Conrad gone, no one says anything.

Caira hasn't spoken to Arriana all week, but Tempe couldn't really care less about the whole thing. What happened with Conrad and Zayne really opened her eyes and made her more accepting.

Tonight is the dinner with my family and Zayne's. I can't help being nervous, so I spend my extra energy cleaning my room, for once. Arriana and my mom just about fainted when they saw my floor cleaned up, desk organized, and even my side of the bathroom counter straightened.

Mom takes Arriana grocery shopping to prepare for tonight, so it's just me and dad.

"You ready for tonight?" he asks as I fuss over making my

bed.

"No," I answer honestly. "He's never seen the house before and I'm really worried I'm going to say or do something stupid and embarrassing."

I flop back on my bed as my dad snickers.

"Tell you what, you cleaned your room so you *must* want the house nice. We'll shock your mom and clean the rest of the house together."

I've never seen my dad clean. I didn't even know he knew how to use a vacuum. After I'm sure he's not joking I get up and find the vacuum.

I start vacuuming my room as my dad sweeps the hard floor in the living room and kitchen. I meet him where the carpet meets the hardwood.

"Do remember meeting mom?" I ask, switching off the vacuum. "Did you do stuff like this when you two started out?"

He stops and props himself on the broom, looking thoughtful.

"When I met your mom, we were in college, she was actually dating my roommate. He was an idiot, like on the verge of getting kicked out of school, idiot. Your mom was way out of his league and her and I would talk when she came by to wait for him. It took maybe two weeks for me to realize how badly I wanted to be with her. Our dorm had never looked so clean after that, the mini fridge we had actually had real food in it. I started caring about what I wore. Over twenty years later, here we are. It's good to care about this stuff, Josh. It shows what you feel is real."

I really do care about Zayne and I really do think I love him. I want this to be real, I want him to see the effort I'm putting in. Maybe it will help him feel safer in his skin to know there's someone who cares this much.

I clean the bathrooms and all the counters and tables while my dad does the dishes. I haven't seen the house look so nice in such a long time. I really hope Zayne and his family like it and feel comfortable.

I look at the time knowing that they'll be here at six. It's almost four. I know my mom is a kitchen wizard and I trust her to get it all done in time, but I'm so afraid that something will go wrong and there won't be time to fix it.

"Oh shit!" I suddenly dart into my room, leaving my dad behind wanting to get on me for my language.

I run into my room and grab the big box by my chair, close it, and hide it in my closet. I breathe a sigh of relief as my dad comes in to see me close the door.

"Hiding stuff in the closet? I thought we were past that," I look to see him smirking at his joke.

"Sorry, I completely forgot I had Zayne's birthday present just sitting in the open. I don't want him to see it."

He nods. "What'd you get him?"

"It's a surprise. I put too much thought into it to let it get spilled by accident." I shrug and give a crooked grin.

We hear the door open and go to meet my mom and Arriana. They look ready to fall over as they put the bags on the counter.

"Geez mom," I say as my dad goes to help carry things in. "It's dinner not a buffet. What are you even making?"

"Not telling, but you'll love it. Did you guys clean? The house looks amazing."

I shove my hands in my pocket, a little giddy. "Yeah, I really want to impress Zayne."

She gives a sweet pout.

"Oh honey, if he isn't impressed with what you've done for him so far, then you've got to find someone else. You have such a big heart."

I leave to let her start prepping to cook. I hear the mixer start up not long after settling into my room. Arriana joins me not long after.

She twirls, showing off her outfit.

"What do you think?" she asks. "Mom let me get a new dress. I think the sweetheart neckline really suits me, don't you?"

"Arriana, I've said it a lot over the years. I may be gay, but that doesn't mean I know what your talking about."

She huffs. "Josh, I swear it's a good thing you don't like girls. You would be hopeless when it comes to helping her pick an outfit."

I chuckle."You do look very nice Arriana, I like it, and I'm sure it will make a good impression."

She beams and twirls again as she walks away. My sister has always been carefully modest in her clothes and this is no exception, her small chest allows her to the "sweetheart neckline" and the thin straps holding the dress up work. The gold that lines the top of her neckline and the bottom of the skirt give it enough wow factor to stand out. It hugs her top while hanging and flowing at her waist. Always simple and well thought out to best represent herself, it's always nice seeing her get so excited.

Arriana leaves both of our doors open and I watch her get ready. She puts on the gold crescent moon necklace I got her for her birthday.

"Arriana, you do know that Zayne and me are gay right?

There are no guys to impress here tonight." I cackle when she glares at me.

"I happen to want to look nice when I finally get to meet his family, and to celebrate what you two have. This is a big deal, Josh. You guys took a big risk and already made a big change."

I hear my phone ring and see it's Zayne.

"Thank god you called, Arriana looks ready for a Milan catwalk, please save me."

She flips me off when she hears me.

"Trust me, my mom is no better." His voice sounds full of life again. "She's been worrying about how to do her hair for almost an hour."

"Her hair is going to be fine no matter what she does."

"See, Mom! Even Josh says it's not a big deal!" I hear him yell.

"How are you feeling today?" I take a serious tone. I've asked him this question everyday and everyday his answer is different.

"I'm ok. My mom was on the phone for almost three hours with Conrad's parents. It was a very mixed conversation. While they don't endorse what Conrad did, they did try to apologize to my parents for their struggle in having a gay son. My mom didn't take it well. It was a mess. I just can't wait to see you. Just talking to you is making today better."

I smile into the phone. "I'm glad that I can help somehow. I'm sorry you had to listen to that. Why was she even talking to the Lewis's?"

"They begged us not to press charges. They kept saying he's young and has such a bright future. My dad sat there going on about how I have the same but Conrad keeps trying to cut it short."

"Zayne, you shouldn't have to listen to them when they're getting into that stuff. Conrad finally got what was coming to him. You need to focus on looking forward. If you ever need to come over to get away from it all you can, we could watch a movie or Arriana could hug you to death."

I hear him chuckle. "Thanks, I think tonight will really help. I want to meet your parents, I want them to like and accept me. I really think it will help."

"Only an hour and a half until you get here, then things will start getting better. I really miss you."

"I miss you too. I've been trying to fill the time and entertain myself. My dad's offered to let me go with him to Target. He and mom want to get some stuff for tonight. I think I might take him up on it."

"You should. I'm not going anywhere and before you

know it you'll be on your way," I look through my closet as we talk.

"Ok, I'll see you later then, and Josh." He pauses. "I love you."

"I love you, too."

We hang up and I feel my smile grow as I take out the shirt I wore when I first kissed Zayne. I change into it and go into the kitchen to help my mom.

I see her putting a cheesecake in the fridge while the ingredients for the rest of dinner sits prepped on the counter.

"Please tell me it's chocolate ripple." I do a little prayer stance.

"Of course, what else? Do you want to help?" She closes the refrigerator door and turns to me. "I could use some help with the rest of this."

I look down to see the many things out, pork chops, potatoes, honey, raspberries. "Mom what are you making?"

"I'm making the pork chops you love so much. Arriana insisted Zayne try the raspberry walnut salad I made last week and I'm also doing honey biscuits and oven roasted potatoes." She beams as she cuts the baby potatoes in half.

"Can I do the pork chops?" I chuckle in excitement as she nods.

Joining her behind the counter I start working, passing the time with jokes and light conversation.

Before I know it, we're taking out all the amazing food and setting the table. I sit anxiously on the couch and wait.

When the doorbell rings I jump up to answer it. I open the door to Zayne and his family. His mom hugs me tight.

My mom comes over to greet them, making small talk with Mrs. Daveen as she hands over wine and apple cider. My dad and Zayne's shake hands and it doesn't take long before they start talking about football and other guy stuff.

We make our way to the table and sit down. Arriana and I sit with Zayne between us while the parents sit on the other side of the table.

"This all looks amazing, Ariel," Mrs. Daveen and my mom talk about cooking and recipe swapping before my mom looks over to me and Zayne, trying to contain her excitement.

"You must be the one I'm hearing so much about." She puts her chin in her hands and stares at us. "It's nice finally meeting the one who keeps my son so happy."

"Mom, seriously?" I start blushing.

They all snicker and Zayne takes my hand under the table. "It's really great to meet you Mrs. Notes. Josh and Arriana spoil me with your food and it's nice to actually get it from the source. Thank you for inviting us."

She nods and everyone starts talking. Dinner flies by as we all laugh and eat, by the time Mom brings out dessert, even our dads look stuffed. They still manage to devour dessert.

We all gather in the living room and watch TV together. Zayne sits with me, his legs lay across my lap, seat-belting me in our chair as he yells possible answers at the game show host.

Seeing all seven of us together, enjoying each other's company so openly, makes my heart warm. It feels really good to have so many people supporting us, and all the openness has definitely helped Zayne. I finally am seeing him smile for real.

We have such amazing families, such an amazing life. Hopefully a long one together.

WAVES OF CHANGE

C ome Monday morning, I spend an extra thirty minutes on the phone with Zayne talking him down from an anxiety attack. Even with Conrad gone, he's scared to go to school. He came over on Sunday to watch a movie with me and catch up on school work he didn't understand. He looked so stressed out and nervous. He woke me up an hour before my alarm when he called me.

"I promise it'll be ok. The whole week you were gone, no one said anything to me or Arri." I rub my eyes. "The most you'll see is some dirty looks." It's not a lie or anything, just not the full truth. I have gotten notes in my locker but Zayne doesn't need to know that.

"That was while I was *gone*, when it was only one of us, and admit it, after everything with Conrad, no one will want to mess with you." His voice is quiet, probably so he doesn't wake up his parents.

"Babe," I stretch out on my bed. "You're the one who gave him a bloody nose and knocked him flat in the cafeteria. If anything, no one will want to mess with you when you get back. Conrad is on the verge of expulsion. He won't do anything when he gets back."

I let out a long yawn that I had been fighting for almost ten minutes. "You're tired aren't you?" Zayne asks. He sounds upset.

"No, I'm ok, do you want me to come over and go to school with you? I can text my mom so she knows I wasn't kidnapped when she wakes up."

I hear a small smirk in his voice. "No it's ok, maybe meet me there, but if you can you should sleep more. I didn't mean to wake you up so damn early."

"Yeah, I always thought you were a little nuts because you are like the first person at school but you hate it the most. Why wake up at ass-crack-dawn when you don't want to be there?"

"I don't really know." I hear the faint creak of his mattress. "Maybe I'll try to go back to sleep with you, arrive barely on time like a normal teen."

I cackle. "Yes, please, sleep. It is calling to us, it draws me in!" I act all dramatic and grin when I hear his giggle.

"Sleep well," I say as he hangs up, only now I can't go back to sleep. Instead I take my shower and get ready early.

While I sit there with all this extra time, I go get the big cardboard box out of my closet and dump everything out. Zayne's birthday is next week and I'm still preparing. Every weekend of waking up to open Church's Chicken and stay until three in the afternoon is starting to pay off. What I don't spend on his birthday is now in a jar in my locked desk drawer for Christmas shopping.

I carefully handle each object and place them in the box, positioning them each in a special way to make it look nice. I still have more stuff I want to get, but I wanted to finally organize this stuff instead of letting it sit unprepared in it's box.

Arriana walks into my room, PJ's rumpled and robe hanging off her. "Josh? What are you doing awake?"

"Zayne got nervous about going back to school so I talked to him for awhile. I couldn't get back to sleep."

She comes up next to me and looks inside the box. "What is all this?"

"Zayne's birthday is next week. I've spent the past month gathering this stuff."

She punches me in the arm. "Why didn't you tell me his birthday was coming up? When is it?"

"Ow! Jesus, you may be small but you are angry!" I rub my arm.

"When's his birthday?"

"November sixth. Jeez, if you're going to do something for him you *do* still have a little over a week."

"I need my present to be better than yours. Tonight I begin!" She then plops on my bed next to the box. "What are we doing for Halloween?"

"What?"

"It's this Thursday, we always dress up." She looks at me like I'm stupid. Rolling her eyes, she puts her hands in front of her, as if she's presenting something. "So I had a couple ideas we can still order online. I kind of already have a few picked out that might include Zayne."

"Arriana, I don't even know if he's into Halloween like we are, I hadn't even thought about it. You can probably do whatever costume you want this year. I think I might just wing it."

She lets out a dramatic gasp, placing her hand to her chest. "How dare you? We aren't related anymore!" She lifts her nose in the air and storms out.

I snicker as I close the box and push it under my bed.

I pass the rest of my time writing and playing on my computer. When it comes time for me to leave, I'm packing my bag when Arriana barges in again.

"He *loves* Halloween and you two are dressing up together. He and I like cop and robber."

"Arriana, what are we going to do Halloween night? We're

gay, most parents here won't let their kids accept candy from us and we won't get invited to parties."

"We'll do scary movie night. Mom and I could make fun snacks. Now the big question. Should I be Little Red Riding Hood, or a Greek goddess?"

"Goddess." I throw my bag over my shoulder, giving her a look of endearment before walking out to the living room.

Arriana and I talk over breakfast while Mom preps a special breakfast sandwich for Zayne. I let her kiss my cheek before leaving to meet him at school.

When I arrive Zayne meets me at the door, looking relieved. I hand him the sandwich and take his free hand. "How are you doing?" I ask.

"I don't know, I'm still nervous."

I drag him along to the direction of the door and walk inside. He tries to resist but I am stronger.

"It's ok," I whisper in his ear.

Walking into the main hall holding hands, we get lots of looks. Most are not nice. When Zayne looks scared I give his hand a squeeze. No one says anything or does anything.

Arriana and Tempe join us quickly. Zayne relaxes into conversation and the day just flows naturally. Tempe and Zayne actually really get along, after Conrad and Zayne's brawl in the cafeteria, she became a little more open minded.

First period is calm and Mr. Roe almost seems to be in an ok mood for once. The day feels long when Zayne and I separate for our other classes, but that's what lunch is for. I'm beyond relieved to see him walk into the cafeteria not scared or beaten up.

In a shocking turn of events, halfway through lunch Caira gets up from her lonely table and asks to talk to Arriana. I don't pretend to not be angry with her for what she said to Arri, I'm definitely not hiding my glare as they walk away. After some major back and forth, they both sit with us. Caira and Arriana agreed that no one has to change their views but they both missed the friendship and will be civil for that. Hopefully Caira can be open minded and see we aren't that bad.

Conversation easily flows back to being lighthearted at the mention of Halloween. Tempe wants to join our movie night and Caira says if we're cool with it, she might make an appearance.

Zayne and her exchange uncomfortable glances every now and then, but after some pushes from Arriana and me, they discover they actually get along and agree on a lot of things. We all make plans for Halloween, picking who will bring what movies, talking about costumes, food, even if we want to try and go out. Together.

Zayne seems tense and unsure, but he and Caira both seem to be approaching with open minds. They're off to a good start building trust. Caira even apologizes for all the times she said mean things or encouraged Conrad's awful behavior.

Lunch ends and we all separate for class, but not before I take a little initiative and send Zayne off with a kiss on the cheek. He blushes, his cheeks as pink as his hair, as he walks down the hall to English. He's so flustered he almost trips looking back at me.

His happiness and energy makes everything feel good inside. Seeing him confident makes everything feel even better.

I sit discreetly on my phone ordering my costume in my wood working class and get excited for Thursday, finally having something that could turn into a real friend group who are willing to try and accept me for me is such a welcomed feeling.

Mrs. Jennings checks on us during the last period, and is happily surprised things are going so well.

"I'll be sure to keep checking in but hopefully we can keep on this path," she says, taking our hands. "Things are really looking up."

The bell rings and the school starts clearing out. Zayne comes home with me and Arriana to work on homework and maybe stay for dinner. He's actually spent a lot of time helping my mom cook, it's encouraged him to get in the kitchen with his mom too. He even had me try a pizza he made from scratch.

I've never seen him so happy, or looking so healthy. His cuts are still there, very slowly healing into scars but to me they've become a symbol of how much he's overcome. Each scar has become an obstacle he's defeated, his eating disorder, the fear of going to conversion therapy, fear of talking things out with his dad, fear of me coming out, fear of Conrad, it's all slowly moving behind him. It's all giving him more strength than I ever thought a person could have. He's gone through so much to earn the huge smile he has now.

Finally, things are getting better.

HALLOWEEN

Walking into school and seeing all the costumes I feel like a kid, except for all the girls in skimpy clothes. Tempe for once doesn't stand out compared to the other costumes, even though her tight, little crayon dress does show off.

Arriana looks fabulous in her soft, flowing goddess dress and sparkling makeup. It takes a lot of me to not cover her with a jacket every time a guy looks at her. She looks great, actually. Her hair is curled perfectly and she put on a body spray that makes her skin shimmer. She put a lot into this and it really paid off.

Zayne comes in in his robber outfit, black pants and a black turtleneck sweater. He has a black beanie over his pink hair and a cheap little mask covering his eyes. He just about drops when I come in in my cop costume. Even though it's not as "sexy" as Arriana wanted, I have to admit I look damn good in it.

I draw him close, whispering in his ears. "Don't make me whip out my cuffs."

He turns beet red as Arriana gags and Tempe looks

hopeful. I smirk at his embarrassment, to see him get so shy is cute.

Arriana spends most of the day handing out candy to classmates. She even slips her number to one of the guys who's been checking her out. Zayne snatches one of her lollipops and just stands next to her as the guy walks off.

"Eh, he's ok," he says, titling his head. "His butt is shaped weird and I think he might be too tall for you. I bet his smells like sandalwood. He looks like a football player, they all smell like sandalwood."

Arriana chuckles as she smacks him in the shoulder. He smirks at her and bites the lollipop.

Tempe and Caira help fix each other's costumes before heading to class. Tempe needs her hat straightened so she actually looks like a sharpened crayon while Caira needs help adjusting her puffy blue Smurfette tutu. I don't get why girls feel the desire to dress revealingly on Halloween, but I guess it makes them happy.

The day drags on with teachers trying to be cool. Mr. Roe almost succeeds with a mad scientist-like thing going on in the classroom and a day of mostly goofy science tricks and pranks. Zayne's English teacher almost makes Edgar Allen Poe work, but breaks character because one kid in his second period class kept playing a recording of a crow on his phone.

Lunch is fun as we all dig into Arriana's candy pile,

basically making it disappear in under fifteen minutes. She frumps at us and rants about how she planned to use the candy to help flirt with the guy from earlier.

"Arriana, I think he's in my class," I say with taffy in my mouth. "Meaning after this summer, he'll probably be far away at college."

"I can hope." She crosses her shimmery arms and pouts at us.

"Girl, I don't think you'll be needing any of this stuff when he's been looking at *you* like candy," Caira jumps in.

"The only candy he'll be touching will be from a pillow sack," I snap.

Arriana gives me a hug. "I love you big brother, even if you are crazy."

I hug back and tell her I will arrest anyone who touches her, earning myself a major stink eye from her *and* Zayne.

"The only people in those handcuffs should be you and me, just saying," he looks me up and down and shakes his head at Arriana.

I lean in close, whispering so only he can hear. "I *should* handcuff you. You *are* a thief, after all, you stole my heart."

He chuckles and takes my hand. He holds on so tight my palm starts sweating.

I think I've gotten the hang of this relationship thing.

The mood at the table shifts when we hear kids at another table laughing. Looking back we see they're laughing at us. Zayne tugs his hand away and puts his head down.

I shoot a glare back at the table behind us and they all shut up. I try to get Zayne to cheer up again, saying they're jealous we have so much candy. I bribe him up with a grape Jolly Rancher, getting him to give a small half hearted snicker.

Arriana, Tempe, Caira, and I all try to keep things light and make Zayne feel better. He's been doing so well and I don't want a few jerks to ruin it. He stays a little reserved but engages in the conversation again until lunch ends and we have to go our separate ways.

Tonight will help, because we'll get to just sit there and I can hold him every time he gets scared during a movie. In an attempt to guarantee him jumping and holding onto me, I insisted we watch The Possession. Arriana insisted we balance the horror with Nightmare Before Christmas, Zayne eagerly agreed with her.

As class drags on I want to get home more and more so I can get things ready for tonight, my mom is making Halloween snacks to help set the mood.

My parents are going to an adult Halloween party at Town Hall, leaving us to do our thing. I think it's a safe bet that tonight there won't be any "fooling around" on behalf of the terror everyone will be feeling.

Once school ends I rush home to bring out the scary cuddle night necessities. I take out the extra comfy pillows from the guest room, glow sticks, some really soft blankets, the softest for me and Zayne because I'm greedy like that, and of course I brought out the secret stash of candy bars for us to stress eat.

My mom goes on about how nice it is that we're all friends and getting along enough to do this, and how she's happy Zayne's doing better.

"I don't know mom, we might scare him to a therapist tonight." I grin mischievously as she gives me a side glare. "I'm kidding."

She and Dad get ready a couple hours later while Arriana and I put the snacks out. Arriana and Tempe picked up a bunch of soda at the dollar store before coming back to the house.

Tempe sits on the couch. "Who do you think will scream first, Zayne or Caira?"

We all look at each other. "I don't know, it depends on what we watch first. If you want Zayne to scream first we should watch *The Possession*. He hates bugs and there's a ton in that movie."

"Caira is terrified of clowns, for her we'd need to watch *It*," Arriana contributes.

We rock-paper-scissors it and I win, leaving Arriana to pout as she sets up the chairs. After everything is done we agree on a movie order and wait for Zayne and Caira to show up.

Caira appears first, also bringing candy, specifically gummy spiders. I pull some aside to tease Zayne with. When he shows up we all settle in. Caira lays on her side on the floor while Tempe and Arriana take the two chairs and Zayne lays on my lap on the couch.

As the movies play, Zayne is the first to scream at the sight of bugs followed by Caira at the sight of a clown popping up. Arriana hides under her blanket and munches popcorn while Tempe mostly dozes off.

Zayne has moved into the crook of my arm and is gripping my shirt tightly as he hides his face in my chest. I let out a content sigh as I stroke his arm, "I've got you."

"Why did I agree to this? I hate you," He mumbles into my shirt.

"I love you, too."

We all jump as Arriana screams and hides completely under her blanket at the sight of the monster in the movie. Zayne doesn't respond much better as he climbs into my lap and bundles in the blanket.

After all the really scary movies when we move to the fun kid ones like *Nightmare Before Christmas* and *Hocus Pocus*, Zayne and Arriana start getting tired from all the excitement and start hesitantly dozing off. Zayne is still clenching my shirt when he falls asleep.

Tempe and Caira both manage to stay awake until the end, quietly saying goodbye as they leave. I hear Caira complain about the clown nightmares she'll have.

With it so quiet and calm, I really look down at Zayne sleeping on me and I reach up to pet his hair. It's still soft as ever.

He must like how it feels because he squirms a little, snuggling into me further as I keep petting his hair. It's comforting having him this close, this vulnerable, this relaxed again. Part of me says to slowly move and lay him on the couch but I don't want to, I don't want this to end.

I look down at where his head lays, straining to look at him resting on my shoulder and I see how cramped he looks in my lap. I want him comfortable, so very slowly and carefully I lay him back on the couch, fixing the pillows to cradle his head. After he's laying down I adjust the blankets to cover all of him and wrap them tightly around him.

I step away slowly and text his mom who's also at the party with my parents.

Zayne is asleep on my couch. Whenever you guys are done and ready you can come get him, let me know so I can wake him

Before disappearing into my room I go back over and give him a light kiss on the forehead. He doesn't even budge.

Leaving to go change, I slip into my room then into my pj pants. Normally I don't wear a shirt but seeing as Zayne is still in my house I feel a little self conscious. I take out a beat up old t-shirt and slip it on as I go back to the living room.

Seeing him and Arriana completely tuckered out makes me tired too, so I take the blankets and pillows Tempe and Caira were using and lay down on the floor beside Zayne.

His hand is sitting by his face and I reach up to grab it, giving a quick squeeze before closing my eyes and drifting off the sleep.

LET GO

I woke up Friday morning in bed and with Zayne gone. Our parents had come home and put us to bed while Zayne's family had gotten him home to do the same. We all spent Friday as slugs. Caira and Tempe even fell asleep in class at one point because they were too freaked out to sleep when they got home.

Normally after school I would have hung out with Arriana or Zayne, but we all kind of had the same idea and ended up going to bed when we got home. None of us did anything until Saturday and even then only Zayne and I went out to do anything.

I took him out to lunch at a Chinese place and let him order whatever he wants in an attempt to create a nice lead up to an awesome birthday in a couple days. Arriana and I have been working on perfecting our gifts. We spent an hour in Target picking wrapping paper, bows, and cards the day after I told her about his birthday.

He has no idea I've planned anything, and I know he wouldn't want me to but he's made a lot of progress and deserves an awesome birthday to celebrate. His mom and my mom are even making him a cake together.

I take him to the mall after lunch and we wander around, spending a lot of time in Hot Topic, given how secure Zayne feels there. I listen to him talk about bands and Disney characters, including the little blue thing I saw him with before school started. He tells me about his little cousin, related to the one he stayed with in Seattle, who loved this stuff. They bonded over this stuff and a love for the color pink. He dyed his hair after she died in a car accident not long after he came out. The little blue character he has was her favorite, the movie it was in was all about family and unconditional love, I can understand why Zayne is so drawn to it.

"Maybe tonight we can watch it together," I put my arm around his shoulder and press my lips to his cheek.

While he wanders the store, I find something I really like and buy it to add to his birthday box.

We walk around a little longer, find the movie for him, and head to my place to settle in for the night. He watches the movie intently and so do I. I was never into Disney, but I like this one. I take a second to look at the DVD box and check out the title to find it online later and maybe even put some stuff from it in his birthday box. *Lilo and Stitch*, I need to remember that.

Zayne stays for dinner and gives us all a quick "thank you" and "goodnight" before meeting his mom in the car to go home. I help my mom clean up and then head to bed.

Waking up on Sunday, I feel sluggish, like I slept but didn't actually sleep. Zayne is out with his family all day, meaning I don't hear from him at all.

I spend my day doing homework and hanging out with my family. Arriana and I finally wrap our presents and everything that night so we can focus on giving him a small party.

Before climbing into bed after dinner that night, I send Zayne a quick text.

I love you. I hope you had a good day and I can't wait to see you tomorrow.

I put up my phone and close my eyes, feeling like my alarm is already ringing a second later. I drag myself out of bed and stretch in agony as I feel the Monday slump settle into me. Arriana is already bouncing around while I sit there dragging my feet and slipping into clothes. I take so long getting ready and eating that my mom insists on driving Arriana and me the short distance to school.

As soon as we get in the front doors I see Zayne. Suddenly I'm wide awake, and not for any good reason. Zayne stands at his locker looking like death warmed over, pale and covered in fresh, still red bruises, a new split in his lip, and dried blood peaking from his nose.

I'm next to him in what feels like half a second. "What the hell happened to you?" I'm steaming mad.

"Josh, I don't--"

"Zayne *what happened?*"

He drops his head and tells me that on his way to school he got knocked to the ground and a group of people put a pillowcase over his head and started holding him down to beat him and yell at him, leaving him in the dirt and gravel as they ran.

"Josh, please." His lips are turned down and his head is tilted to the side. "I don't have the energy to fight this today."

"Mrs. Jennings is going to check on you and find out!"

"It didn't happen at school, she can't do anything."

He looks so tired and desperate. I hate the thought of him covered in bruises on his birthday, I quickly yank him into a tight hug, clenching my jaw as tight as I try to keep quiet.

We get to first period to see Conrad, back from his suspension, with a smug grin. "Got a bit of a boo boo there Zayne?"

I start to charge at him, Zayne holds me back and begs me to just sit down. I begrudgingly listen. My eyes never leave Conrad though and I feel my temperature rise in my anger.

Zayne and I part ways at the bell, and he hides in the bathroom during lunch. He promises me he's eating and asks to be left alone for a bit. I don't see him the rest of the day, only getting a few texts of reassurance.

Mrs. Jennings did find out, and even though she can't do anything to the people who attacked him, she says she'll try and find evidence of who did it.

Arriana and I discuss it at home as I go under my bed to slide out his wrapped box of gifts.

"What are you doing?" she asks, looking over my shoulder.

"I can't let him sit at home miserable. His mom grocery shops on Mondays and his dad works, so he's home alone with this stuff on his mind."

I ask my mom if I can borrow her car as I carry the long box into the living room. She offers to help me open the trunk and take me to his apartment. My phone starts ringing.

I try to balance the box in my arms as my mom unlocks and opens the trunk. The box starts wobbling, threatening to fall out of my arms.

It's Zayne.

I know I'll be there in fifteen minutes at most and I need to get this box in the car, so I let it go to voicemail for the first time.

I climb in the passenger seat and my mom starts driving, I tell her what happened while we drive.

The ten minute drive comes to a screeching halt as I see spray paint and eggs splattered all over the front of Zayne's apartment.

"Oh my Lord!" My mother looks appalled as I jump out and run up the steps, leaving the box in the car.

I wiggle the doorknob, trying to get it open. "Zayne! Zayne are you in there?"

I find the spare key again, unlocking the door as fast as I can. I don't think anything could have prepared me for what I found. The apartment is destroyed, pictures broken, books ripped, broken dishes in shards on the floor.

"Zayne?" I rush to his room. It takes me a few moments to process what I see before dropping down on my knees.

Zayne's lying on his floor, and blood is everywhere.

"Zayne!" I grab him and tug him close. He's completely limp in my arms. "Wake up Zayne!" He doesn't move or say anything. I feel panic and fear set in as I try to cover his bleeding arms. "Mom!" I start screaming at the top of my lungs and sobbing as she comes in the front door to see the apartment in disarray.

"Oh God!" She runs over and whips out her phone to call for help.

I scream and beg Zayne to open his eyes. I watch my mom

yank off her belt and tighten it around Zayne's upper arm. She finds another belt on top of his dresser to use on his other arm.

My cheeks burn and my shirt is stained dark red. I hear sirens approaching, but I can't look away.

Paramedics rush in. They ask me to step back but I can't let go. My mom and a police officer have to drag me away screaming.

"Zayne!" The tears fall faster than I thought possible, I watch him grow farther away as they drag me out the door. "Zayne!"

We sit outside a couple minutes, me clinging to my mother as she holds me and calls Zayne's mom.

Suddenly I look up and see the paramedics carrying Zayne out of his apartment on one of those body boards. They have him strapped down and have bandages soaked in blood covering his arms.

They load him into the ambulance and I try yet again to get to him, meeting resistance from police officers.

"Let me go!" I'm screaming like a mad man. I sound like Zayne did when he beat up Conrad, "Let go of me! Zayne!"

My mom tugs me back, holding me close as they close the ambulance doors and take off down the street. Not long after it leaves, Zayne's parents arrive. Their car looks like it's been keyed.

"Where is he? Where's my baby?" Mrs. Daveen is hysterical. She begs officers for answers when she sees me, "Josh! What happened? Where is he?"

I can't breathe. My mom drags me behind her and takes Mrs. Daveen's hand to explain what we came here to find. Mr. Daveen joins her, listening closely and catching his wife as she falls to her knees sobbing.

The police insist on asking questions but all I want is to get to the hospital, as does everyone else. I answer their questions as fast as I can. I tell them how we found the apartment, that the door was locked, I tell them Zayne very well might have done this to himself and honestly might not have been attacked, causing this massive bleeding.

"They beat him and then they do this? He didn't ask for this, how do people get away with blindfolding a kid and beating him on the street just to come and vandalize his home?" His father is livid as they let us go and we all take off for the hospital.

Mom calls Dad and Arriana, telling them what happened. I don't hear anything though, all I do is see and smell. The metallic smell of Zayne's blood is soaked into my shirt and I feel like my chest is heaving out of control. We arrive at the E.R. and are told to wait in the waiting room until the doctor has more information.

We sit there, my mom holding me as my dad and sister show up. Arriana is bawling as she goes to hug Mrs. Daveen.

"He called me," I whisper, tears still stinging my eyes.

"What honey?" My mom leans in close.

"He called me mom, right before we left. He called me and I didn't answer." My breathing speeds up and I start to tremble. "Why didn't I pick up the phone? Why couldn't I pick up the goddamn phone? If only I had picked up!" I start getting hysterical.

My dad holds my mom back as I jump up and hit a wall. Mrs. Daveen approaches me and yanks me over to her.

"Josh honey, this isn't your fault. The only people to blame are those who hurt him and destroyed the house. If you hadn't been there we would be crying at the morgue instead of in the E.R.. Josh you gave him a fighting chance. This is *not* your fault!"

I grab her arms, Zayne's blood dry on my skin, and just start sobbing again. She sits me down and we huddle together.

We sit there for over an hour before a doctor comes out to talk to us. We all jump up seeing him. All I see is the blood on his scrubs.

"He's stable." We all breathe a sigh of relief. "He's still unconscious but we stopped the bleeding and have given him more blood. He did manage to damage some muscles in his wrist but hopefully he can make a full recovery. We're moving him to a room then you can see him."

The doctor looks to Zayne's parents.

"Once he wakes up we have to perform a psychiatric evaluation and keep him on a suicide watch. It's a mandatory 24 hour period here under extreme supervision. It could be longer depending on his evaluation. I'll take you to see him if you'd like."

We all follow closely behind. When we get to his room, I can't go in. I sit outside his door, and I just lose it, letting the tears finally escape.

He's alive.

Thank god he's alive.

RETRIBUTION

My dad took Mom and Arriana home so they could rest and get changed. He brings me fresh clothes while I stay with Zayne's parents to be here when he wakes up. It's almost three in the morning when he starts stirring.

The three of us jump up as his eyes flutter open. His mom races to his side.

"Momma?" His voice is raspy and dry.

"Oh my baby." She starts weeping as she runs her hand over his head, a small smile and euphoric chuckle escape her as she takes his hand tightly. "I thought I lost you."

Tears well up in all of our eyes, even Zayne's. His parents hold his hands tightly and throw all the love they have at him. Slowly, I step forward. He sees me and his face becomes one of despair.

"Josh, I..." He starts to tremble lightly as I come to his bedside.

I look at him for a second, taking in that he's alive, and suddenly start bawling. I reach over and hug him tightly, not caring about the bedrail pressing into my stomach.

"I thought you were dead, I was so scared," I whisper as I hold his hospital gown in my fists. He returns my hug.

"I'm so sorry, Josh. I'm so sorry. I didn't know what to do." He starts crying too. "Everything was happening so fast and I got scared and I thought it was all my fault. When you didn't answer I thought something had happened and you were ignoring me."

I pull him tighter into my hug.

"Don't ever think that!" I breathe. "I would never ignore you. I was coming to cheer you up. I had no idea about your apartment, I found you lying there and I didn't know what to do. I was so scared you were going to die right on that floor."

We hold each other until the doctors come for his evaluation. I get sent home to sleep, even though I know I can't.

Come morning, I'm still awake and I go to school just so I don't sit at home worried. The school has been made aware of what's happened and that Zayne's evaluation makes it clear he needs to be under constant watch for close to three weeks. The police link with the school to try and find the culprit, thinking it's connected to the bullying at school. The school throws together an assembly to alert the student body to what has happened and the consequences.

Mrs. Jennings explains the police presence and assures the school that if anyone is tied to these incidents, there will be very severe punishments. She then invites me up to talk about Zayne's condition and the situation, as his parents wanted to be at the hospital with him.

I step up to the microphone and stare at the crowd. All the anger and fear bubbles inside of me, "At four forty five last night, I discovered Zayne Daveen lying in a pool of his own blood in the ruins of his apartment. Yesterday morning, I came to school to find him beaten mercilessly, all because he doesn't fit the cookie cutter mold."

"Because of the ignorance and cruelty many people, many in this very room, inflicted on him *daily* he attempted to take his own life. As he lay there dying, what would have been his final thought, wasn't that he was finally giving into the hatred that was spewed at him, it wasn't the hope that the pain would end...it was disgust in himself, thinking he brought this on his family and friends by being himself."

"Those of you who brought him to this, who *do* think he brought this on himself, I hope you know how disgusted so many of us are with you. Not me, nor his family or mine would change Zayne for anything. We would rather happily stand by him and face the cruelty you force on us than tell him to change and surrender to you." Rage builds up in me as I watch the crowd, some look horrified, some look bored, I even see some roll their eyes. I can't tell what's bubbling inside me, strength? Fear?

Frustration? Whatever it is, it comes out full force and I don't hold back, "You have accomplished nothing but bringing attention to what you have done, you've accomplished nothing but hurting a family that did nothing to you. I can speak for those in that waiting room that night, I can tell you how long we cried, afraid we would never see him again. I can tell you the fear we faced until near dawn, waiting to see if he would wake up. I can tell you, that in the end, you accomplished *nothing*. Zayne is now recovering, and with the hell you're bringing down on yourselves, and the number of people standing with him, you have no chance of beating him." I watch as everyone *really* starts paying attention, in awe and shock. They're finally listening, I'm going to make sure they *keep* listening! "Never again will any of you lay a finger on him, never again will any of you force your harsh words on him, because now..." I make eye contact with Conrad, seeing the fear and anger on his face, I can't help but smile, "Now he has the resources to finally tear you down and become stronger that you will *ever* hope to be."

I leave the stage and the auditorium to go sit in the office, still fuming mad while also feeling numb. It feels like I'm watching everything happen, not actually experiencing it. My heart races and my mind can't focus on anything. Mrs. Jennings comes over and puts a hand on my shoulder, offering to call my mom to take me to the hospital. I take the offer graciously as I cool down.

I get there while Zayne is sleeping, so I slide one of the

room chairs over by his bed and wait. That is where I stay until his birthday.

That day, I leave when he sleeps after breakfast to go to the car, hauling out the box that was left there since I found him on the floor of his room. Tonight, he goes to the psych ward for his three weeks. There will be visitation, but it won't be the same as getting to stay by his side during this process.

I bring the box to his room, surprising him when he wakes up. By that time Arriana has joined me with her gift. I see the corners of his mouth turn up weakly, but it's real joy he's showing. He opens her present first and chuckles at the iTunes gift cards, books, and candy. He gives her a hug before turning to my box.

"Is it sex toys? Or the handcuffs?" He smirks and claps, making us all chuckle as he opens the box and stares in amazement.

He takes out a framed copy of my mom's chocolate chip cookie recipe, a special gay pride T-Shirt that reads **Everything is Pride...And Equality Matters!** It's signed by the band that released the shirts. He keeps taking things out, like the item I bought while he wasn't looking at Hot Topic. I watch his eyes fill with tears as he looks at the pack of matching rings on chains. The packaging talks about how wearers pledge to be allies to the LGBT+ community, but to also wait to get married until federal, state, and worldwide laws allow marriage equality for all.

Zayne tugs me into a deep kiss before digging deeper into the box, bringing out sheet music for violin for some of his favorite songs, as well as a little plushy like the one Lilo had in *Lilo and Stitch*. I even got him a Stitch throw blanket. I bring out the last present, my old iPod, loaded with all of his favorite songs. I wrap him in the blanket and skip to the last song.

He holds me closer as we listen to Calum Scott's "No Matter What." I tell him that we will be here no matter what for him and he starts sobbing.

His parents join us and he shows them his presents. Together, we wait for the doctors to come take him to his room for the next three weeks.

His mom holds the stuff they won't let him take as they put him in a wheelchair and roll him away. I hold his hand down the hall until it's time to let go, and even then I want to just hold him close.

I watch him disappear into the elevator, still wrapped in the blanket, holding the shirt. His parents meet me in the hall.

"Things are going to get better now, hopefully this will help him." His dad puts his hand on my shoulder. "He'll be home before we know it. Thank you for saving our boy, Josh, and thank you for doing so much for him."

I nod as we go to get Arriana and leave for the night.

Arriana and I are tasked with getting Zayne his missed schoolwork and then coming back here for visiting hours so we need to be asleep early.

It's hard not being able to text Zayne or call him to ask if he's ok. Most nights, I toss and turn waiting for the time to pass. I've played every video game I own, and even found new ones. I've paced holes in the floor wondering if he's ok. I took extra shifts at work. I've looked at every book and magazine in the house to try and distract myself. I even spent three days writing a story about a world where the oppressed are given powers to fight injustice. Everything I can do to pass the time, I've done, none of it helps...

The only thing that helps me is hearing that final bell at school and knowing that that means I'm going to see him.

Arriana often joins me. Mom and Dad even join us sometimes. Mom especially is having a hard time after seeing Zayne and me like that.

Today it's just me though. Today is the second to last day before he comes home. I want to see him, tell him things will get better, I want to be able to kiss him again. More than anything, I want him to be able to come home and feel safe again.

Watching Arriana get in Ciara's car, I make my way to my

bike. She wanted to come, but I need to see him, I need to be with him alone for once. I can see him trying to put on a brave face for everyone when they visit. I just have to hope I can break through. None of us want him falling back into his dark place because he was too scared to be real with us. I won't lose him. He *will* know that he isn't alone and that we're here for him no matter what.

The bike ride is long and almost painful, but I couldn't care less. The thought of seeing Zayne is enough to make me cross an ocean. He's seemed so different since he went in there. I think it freaks him out in there. Everytime I see him, he avoids talking about anything going on in there, instead he asks about my writing or Arianna and school.

Pedaling faster than I ever have before, I'm greeted by the sight of the hospital. I'll see him in just a few moments. It's all I can think about. Just a little longer.

"He knows he only has one day left after today, that's got to cheer him up. It's going to be ok," I mumble to myself as I make my way through the hospital door.

I don't need to look at signs anymore. I know where I'm going. The psych ward is on the fifth floor, and I don't have any hesitation walking up to the desk. I'm greeted by a nurse's bubbly attitude. It's the same nurse as the past few days. She's not surprised to see me.

"Hey Denise," I lean on the counter as she taps on her

computer.

"Hi Josh, he's in group right now. They should be done in maybe ten minutes. Do you want to wait out here?"

I shake my head, "I'll head down to the vending machine really quick. The bike ride was a serious workout. Do you want anything?"

"Oh honey, you're too sweet! If they have any pretzels, I'd love a bag. Thanks dear!"

I nod and I make my way back down the hall, stopping in front of a line of vending machines. Candy, chips, drinks, and other snack foods sit on display in front of me. I shove the dollar into the machine and get a bag of pretzels while I weigh my options. A Gatorade sounds good right now, but I need food too. I can't focus on anything as I find the clock on the wall, watching the minutes tick by. Grumbling to myself, I get my drink and one of those cheap prepackaged peanut butter and jelly sandwiches.

Denise is still focused on the computer as I walk past, placing the pretzels on the counter. Her smile is contagious, and I can't help but smile back as I sit down, tapping my foot impatiently.

"He seemed to be doing really well today, if that helps at all," she tells me. "Seeing you always helps, too."

A chuckle escapes me as I feel my lips turn up. I wait,

eating and watching the clock. Seconds feel like hours. Then, I hear a faint buzz on the other side of the waiting room doors. Glancing up, I see Denise nod to me.

"Go on kiddo, visiting hours."

She lets me through the door leading to a set of tables. Each table has a chess board. I've never seen anyone use them. Taking a seat, I wait and run my hands through my hair. It's getting long. I should get it cut soon.

My attention is drawn to the door across the room as a couple of kids, some younger than me, walk in. Zayne is with them. He looks tired, but he's smiling. The closer he gets, the clearer his exhaustion becomes. He has bags under his eyes and his hair is a mess. He sits down across from me.

"Hey." I keep my voice a low whisper as I reach out for his hand. He's shivering.

"I missed you."

"You saw me yesterday, but I missed you too. Are you alright? You look..."

Zayne shrugs his shoulders. "Just really tired, the doctors and staff are great, but they can't really fix homesickness. I don't like sleeping here, it doesn't feel right."

"I'm sorry babe...has being here helped otherwise? We haven't really talked about your stay since you got admitted.

Do you *want* to talk about it?"

"I don't mind it. Group therapy helps a bit. Dr. Zolla is amazing. I wasn't keen on the hospital food so one of the nurses has me tell her what I will eat and she goes and gets it for me." A snicker escapes him, one of the first ones I've heard in over a week. "Dr. Zolla says I'm doing well though, and told me the homesickness is normal. At least I get to go home soon."

"One more night after tonight, then you'll be in your bed again. You'll be home. Is Dr. Zolla going to still be your doctor after you leave?"

"I think so. I like her, and so do Mom and Dad. She's nice, and she doesn't judge me. It was hard the first couple of days. Opening up to her didn't come easy but she told me something that kind of just clicked in me."

I squeeze his hand as he starts to stare off. "What's that?"

"It's ok to not be ok."

Looking at him as he says that, I see a sense of calm overtake him. I feel it too. I let him tell me all about therapy and how he's been feeling, I listen to him talk about the coping mechanisms his doctor taught him.

"You know your mom has a big dinner planned for when you get out," I tell him. "We all miss you, and we're all proud of you."

"She doesn't have to do anything special." I can see his ears turn as pink as his hair.

"Are you kidding? The world should be throwing you a parade after what you've been through. We miss you, and we're dumb lucky to still have you." Zayne stares at me with wide eyes and I feel my heart melt. "God I love you and your selfless, no-attention-on-me attitude. You don't see how much love and attention you deserve."

I see the corners of his lips twitch. He wants to be excited, but he is still nervous and uncomfortable with the idea of all this attention, so I change the subject. Dragging my bag onto my lap, I take out my journal and show him a couple of short stories I wrote for him.

We talk for what feels like minutes and forever at the same time. I tell him I'm looking into journalism courses for college and talk about starting a blog. He talks about how he doesn't know what he wants to study. He asks how Arianna, Ciara, and Tempe are doing. We talk about school and our parents. My hand never leaves his as we pass the time.

I can feel my heart sinking when they announce visiting hours are over. Squeezing his hand, I press my lips to his cheek and ignore the ache in my chest.

"I'll be right here waiting for you. Just two more days." I struggle to let go of him. "I love you."

Time flies and before I know it, it's time for Zayne to come home. No more visiting hours, no more tossing and turning wanting to call him, no more missing him. He's coming home, he's finally coming home.

I go with everyone to pick him up. Even Tempe and Caira join us to greet him at his discharge. We all bring him home and work to get him settled at home again.

The apartment has been cleaned and the front repainted. It almost looks normal again. It's a clean slate, a fresh start to move forward.

Word of Zayne's recovery travels fast and it's obvious who reacts unhappily to that news. There have been no confessions yet, but I have my suspicions. People are still uncomfortable with Zayne and me together, but now no one says anything. Notes still appear in our lockers and sometimes our mail, but we just throw them away. We're not going to let them get to us again.

You see some people are disappointed with how things turned out and honestly, I love it, seeing the faces of those to blame for this situation and seeing them acknowledge to themselves that they've lost feels amazing.

They did lose.

For once, we win.

Recovery

Zayne comes back to school earlier than expected. After Thanksgiving break ends, he's right there in that classroom ready to get back to life. He has stitches in his arm that people stare at, but soon they'll be gone.

Since his suicide attempt, Zayne has been living life more. He's been going out more and coming over more. He's doing better in school, too.

By December, his stitches are gone, but scars remain. Every now and again I see them and get scared all over again, but I drag myself into reality and see how much better he's gotten.

His parents have him in therapy, and he admits that he's glad to be here. He's even glad it happened. Without this event, he wouldn't have seen just how much he was losing with his life. Without this, he wouldn't have finally won in the battle against the ignorance in our school.

I often catch him stopping on the way home from school just to stand and enjoy the sun. He's pushed me to go out more too, so he and I often go out to eat or go on drives on the weekend. Every day I see more of him come alive. I see this side of him I never knew. He's happy.

It's incredible.

Zayne asked me to meet him at my locker when school got out. As I approach, I see him with his earbuds in listening to the iPod I gave him. The way his eyes light up at the sight of me makes my heart melt.

Taking out his earbuds, he draws me seductively into a hug. "Are you alright?" I ask, embracing the hug.

"You need to stop asking me that everytime you see me. I'm great." He chuckles as he takes my hand. "You ready?"

"For what?"

"We're going out for the night, just us! Let's go."

As he tugs me out through the front door, I bring him closer, wrapping my arm around his shoulders. "You know I love you, right?"

He stops at his dad's station wagon, taking a moment to nuzzle his face against my neck.

"Of course I know that, I love you too." He kisses my cheek before whipping out the keys for the car. "Come on."

Climbing in the car, I see his wrists and the scars that cover them. I can't help myself, I reach out and place my hand on his leg. It feels stupid but I need to prove he's still here, that the cheeky grin on his face is real, that he's still mine.

Zayne keeps chatting away, oblivious to my action or concerns, "My mom says 'hi' by the way, she was a bit sad when I said we wouldn't see her tonight, but I think she'll recover. How was the rest of your day?"

"It was ok, I'm ready for Winter break. I'm ready to just spend time with you and my family and everyone, you know?"

"Yeah, honestly, I can't wait for Christmas. I think you'll like what I got you!" His joy warms every part of me.

"You didn't have to get me anything." I squeeze his leg, "I have you, what else could I ever need?"

He takes my hand. I let my mind wander as I watch him, occasionally looking at the passing scenery.

I think we're heading to Dallas, but I'm not sure, so I just enjoy the ride and listen as Zayne sings along to the radio. He's actually really good. Listening to him sing is really soothing.

"How's violin practice been?" I ask after a while.

Zayne stops singing and glances over at me. His violin is the one thing he's still really struggling with. He damaged some of the muscles in his wrist, and getting back that strength is hard.

"It's getting better, depending on the song I can get most of the notes right," he answers. "The hard part is having the strength for a full song. The doctors are impressed with my progress though. They said it should take longer than it is."

"You'll get there, you never cease to amaze us all."

I watch his cheeks turn an adorable shade of red as he focuses on the road again. Watching him, I let my mind travel. I still think about that night at the park, our first kiss, our weekends in the city, him curled up in my lap on Halloween, how it feels to hold his hand...

I don't think anything could ever compare to being with him.

The drive is calm and quiet. I find myself dozing off along the trip. Car naps are so comforting, even more so when you wake up to the face of someone you love.

"Hey," Zayne whispers, squeezing my hand. "You awake?"

"I am now." I feel my lips turn up in a sleepy grin.

He leans in to kiss me. The sensation wakes me up instantly and we climb out of the car together. I'm unable to keep my hands off him as I draw him close and look around. We've arrived at the same Waffle House I took him too before going to the support group a couple months ago. He and I still go to the meetings every month, and often go out and hang out with the people we've met, like Devin. We've made a few friends and they all help and support Zayne in his recovery.

"I hope you're hungry," Zayne says, wrapping his arms

around me, luring me forward.

"I'm always hungry when it comes to you." I don't pretend not to find pleasure in making him horny and embarrassed.

"You're horrible, you know that?" He draws me into a kiss and I feel every part of me give in.

My hands run up into his black and pink hair, still soft as ever. I can't help let my fingers travel down his face and body, feeling every muscle and inch of him. He's started working out and eating more, he's not the same scrawny guy he was in August. Now he's so fit and strong and confident and it's just so incredibly sexy. Confidence looks so good on him.

"Alright..." His voice is a soft mumble against my lips. "Let's get inside before you start stripping me."

I start snickering as we walk inside. It's not very busy. I count maybe five full tables as we take a seat. Zayne sits across from me in the booth and starts looking at the menu, focus taking over and making his face scrunch up in the cutest way.

I'm so lucky he's still here.

I don't realize he's talking to me until he's shaking my arm. "Josh? Babe? You sure you're alright?"

Shrugging him off, I try to give a smirk and stop thinking of all the bad stuff. Wrapping my fingers in his I try to focus on what's in front of me.

"I'm great, I'm sorry, my head's just in a different place right now."

"You know you can tell me if something is going on, right?"

"Of course. I know that. It's nothing, I promise."

"Josh," He squeezes my hand, his face becoming serious. "You don't have to walk on eggshells around me. I'm doing ok. I don't need to be coddled, if something is wrong I want to help."

"Zayne, don't do that. I'm ok."

Nothing in his expression has changed. He doesn't like that we all worry about him so much. He doesn't want us to fuss. In his mind, we shouldn't focus on what could happen, we should focus on his progress, but he acts like he doesn't still have bad days.

Some days, he still looks like crap and seems to fall right back to where he was months ago. Sometimes a hate note will appear in his locker or in the mail, some days he tries to play his violin and falls into a dark place when he can't. It's hard to focus on only the good when all this is still happening. It won't all go away overnight.

"Dr. Zolla says internalizing isn't healthy," Zayne tells me gently. "It's not good to try and carry all the negative weight yourself. You can't fix it all on your own. Let me in, Josh.

Please."

He begs me with his eyes. I can see the desperation. His lips are turned down as he stares back at me with his adorable amber eyes. I can't say no to him.

With a sigh, I lean back.

"I just worry," I explain. "I can't help but think about how different things could have turned out. If I had just picked up the phone that night, or if I had gotten there a few minutes sooner...if I had gotten there just a few minutes *later*..." My heart squeezes at the thought. "I could have lost you, I worry I still could! This stuff...the bad stuff won't just go away and we were all scared we'd never see you again. We're all scared you could fall back into *that* place! You act like everything is all better, and we can't help but be scared for another bad day or an extreme shift when things *aren't* better anymore."

His eyes stay glued to mine for a moment before he looks away. I can see him biting the inside of his cheek. What I would give to know what he's thinking, he looks hurt, or upset, I can't really tell.

"Please say something," I beg.

"I *am* doing better Josh, I really am. I don't want you guys to always worry about me."

"We know you're doing better! We're so proud of you, but that doesn't mean you're always going to be doing better. You can't pretend the bad days don't exist. We worry because we *love* you, we want you to be safe and we don't want to lose you. You just told me your doctor says *not* to internalize things. You don't need to hide when you have a bad day."

I get up and sit next to him in the booth, running my fingers down the back of his head. I watch his eyes close. My heart pounds in my chest waiting for any type of reaction. The silence is deafening. Trying to focus on nothing but the soft feeling of his hair on my rough fingers, I make an attempt to show him that I'm here for him.

"I'm not pretending they don't exist," he finally says. "I just *wish* they didn't. I don't like still feeling like I'm in that place. More than anything, I want to be better and be past all that."

I take his chin in my hand, enticing his lips to mine for a moment, "You *have* come so far, and you'll go even farther if you're honest about how you're doing. Remember what Dr. Zolla told you when you first started seeing her?"

He nods, pressing his forehead to mine. "It's ok to not be ok."

"It's ok to not be ok." I recite it with him a few times as he holds my hand, neither of us caring about the pain from holding so tight.

I let him rest his head on my shoulder as we look over the

menu together.

We order our food and keep talking as we wait. He asks me about my games and writing, asking if I've reconsidered my English teacher's recommendation of entering my writing in contests. He says it will look good to any writing programs I apply for at college. I shrug him off, not sure if I want to put myself out there like that. Instead I turn the conversation back to him, I do anything I can to make him laugh. His laugh is incredible. He doesn't like it. He thinks he sounds ridiculous and loud, but I think it's like a symphony of happiness erupting with life.

His eyes sparkle when the food comes. Before I move back across the booth, I take some of the whipped cream with my finger and put in on his nose, earning a mischievous but genuine smile. With a few dirty jokes, I get him blushing and I feel myself relax.

Christmas decorations are already up everywhere. Music pours out of the speakers and I feel the holiday spirit fill me. This is my first Christmas out of the closet, my first one in a relationship...it's my first Christmas with Zayne.

"What would your family normally do around this time of year?"

He looks stunned. "We kind of just do what everyone else does, we exchange gifts and eat and watch Christmas movies. Only thing that's changing this year is it shouldn't be as awkward this year. What about you?"

"It all would depend on if my dad was on a business trip, there were years where he'd be away so we wouldn't celebrate until he got back. We usually make cookies together, mom makes a big dinner, maybe if we feel up to it we'll drive around and look at Christmas lights around town."

"It'll be nice spending the holiday together, maybe starting our own traditions."

I nod and keep making small talk. Zayne seems so excited for the holiday, it finally feels like everything is coming together and getting better. This is going to be one of the best Christmases ever.

Make the Yuletide Gay

Music floods the room, I can hear my mom chuckling in the living room as my dad helps her finish putting together the pile of gifts under the tree. Arriana is in her room getting ready all while I just sit staring at my ceiling. I feel so cynical, thinking of what if's and being so paranoid but I feel I can't calm down until I see Zayne with my own eyes.

He's definitely getting better, but he still has bad days. I glance at my clock. It's almost noon, he should be here soon. I tap my finger on the corner of my laptop, trying to work on a story to keep my mind off everything, and I'm totally failing. I've maybe written ten words, and spent an hour staring at the screen worrying about Zayne.

"You alright in here?" Arriana draws my attention as she stands in the bathroom doorway.

"Just thinking, today could be going a very different way." I look back up to my ceiling.

"Josh... Josh, please look at me?" I let my eyes meet hers. "It's ok, Zayne is ok."

I know she's right. I know I'm just being paranoid. Zayne

would tell me if something was wrong, he's been better about that too. It's just this feeling of dread I have won't seem to go away.

"Did you talk to him today?" Arriana asks.

"Yeah, of course I did."

"And?... Was there any reason to worry?"

I roll my eyes, "I get your point. He just...he had a tough day yesterday."

"We all know the tough days will still happen. How bad was it?"

I shrug and think back to how he sounded on the phone. "Maybe a seven out of ten. He sounded exhausted and distant. He tried to practice the violin and couldn't do it. It's very discouraging to him."

"He knows it will take time. Imagine how great he'll feel when he can play again."

"Let's take it one day at a time. I just want to see him."

She yanks me close and into a hug. "Yeah, I know, so do I. I want to see his face when he opens my *clearly* superior present!"

I shove her playfully, telling her she's full of crap, then send her out so I can put on some decent clothes. Her red dress bounces as she runs off, looking as perky and excited as usual.

I hope I look alright as I put on some dark jeans and a green shirt. I've never been good with clothes, but now I at least try. Mom and Arriana have definitely noticed.

Deciding to busy myself, I help my mom set up the cookie station, still watching the clock obsessively. Time moves slowly, I try not to think about it as I talk to my dad. I feel my heart skip in my chest when the doorbell finally rings.

"I'll get it!" I call as I cross the living room at a superhuman speed. I pretend I don't hear my parents chuckling.

Opening the door, I feel the involuntary smile come across my face. Seeing him always takes my breath away.

I'm brought back to reality when his mom ropes me into a hug. "Oh Josh! Good to see you honey, merry Christmas!"

"Merry Christmas Mrs. Daveen, it's good seeing you too. Please come in!"

I step to the side and let her pass me. She hands me a box before darting over to my mother. Zayne's dad isn't far behind her as he passes me with a quick handshake and greeting. He and my dad talk as he puts down a bunch of other boxes he was carrying.

I look back to Zayne who just stands there watching me. He looks so tired, but he seems happy.

Drawing him close, I run my hand down his cheek. "Merry

Christmas, Zayne."

"Merry Christmas." I stop thinking as he wraps his fingers around mine and kisses my cheek.

After a few moments, I realize we're still standing in the doorway, so I tug him along and into the living room where my family swarms him with hugs and small talk.

I sit on the couch and watch him light up. He looks so happy as he stands around looking at the decorations and talking about presents and Christmas movies. Eventually he comes to sit with me, draping his legs over my lap. I finally give myself the chance to take in how he looks.

He has bags under his eyes but his excitement and joy is genuine. Of course I almost don't notice anything else after seeing his obviously ugly Christmas sweater, complete with glitter and garland and reindeer.

"I'm digging the shirt babe." I chuckle as I squeeze his leg.

He runs his hand through his hair, clearly embarrassed, but it's cute.

"Call it a moment of whimsy. Is it that bad?"

"It's adorable."

I see him relax. Together, he and I try to pick a holiday movie to put on while my mom brings out frosting for cookie decorating. It's Mom's favorite tradition. We can all do something together and then all join in the living room to watch movies and open presents.

Zayne sees the cookies and sprinkles and gets excited. It doesn't take him long to bounce from his seat and start tugging my arm. Both of us giggle as I drag myself off the couch and to the counter where we find a number of colors, shapes, decorations, and cookies.

I sit back and decorate a tree and watch how happy everyone is. Arriana and Zayne fight over the pink sprinkles while our parents drink wine and try to create more intricate designs on their cookies. I listen as they all chatter away, discussing gifts and plans for the new year.

"Maybe we can all go to prom together!" Arriana's eyes light up as Zayne and I stare at her.

We hadn't even thought about prom. Zayne never really seemed interested. I mean, yeah he's doing better and is being more open at school, but social events still freak him out. I sort of just expected us to stay in that night.

"Maybe we can." Zayne's words surprise me, but his smirk washes away all hesitation.

I won't pretend it doesn't excite me, the idea of dressing up and picking him up, spending a night as normal teens and not giving two shits what others think. Now it just depends which of us will be first to ask the other.

I focus on my cookie again, listening to him and Arriana talk about the gifts they got for Ciara and Tempe. They take turns trying to guess what's inside the gifts under the tree.

My mom and Mrs. Daveen start chuckling as I roll my eyes. "Guys," I chastise them. "In like twenty minutes, you'll open them and you won't have to guess." I mimic my mind exploding as Arriana gives me a dirty look and Zayne giggles, getting up from his seat.

"Where's the fun in that?" Zayne stands next to my seat, resting his head on my shoulder.

"The surprise and satisfaction when you finally open it."

I see his eyes sparkle. He's glowing. Seeing him have this much fun makes it all feel right. He's teasing me. He's joking around. I absolutely love it.

"He just knows that I know what he got you! He doesn't want me to spoil it, he also doesn't want me to spoil that my gift is so much better!" Arriana gives us a mischievous grin as she pours some of the sprinkles in her mouth.

"Arriana Maria Notes! Don't you dare eat all the sprinkles!" My mother's voice carries over everything, causing all of us to burst into laughter.

Zayne leans against me, clutching his stomach as he snorts and chuckles. "Maria?! Your middle name is *Maria*?"

I watch my sister turn lobster red, although, I can't tell if it's from anger or embarrassment. Whatever it is, it makes us cackle louder. While my mother goes to hug her and apologize, Zayne and I make a special pink Christmas tree cookie to apologize for laughing.

We all gather the cookies and settle in the living room, *A Christmas Story* plays faintly in the background as we start passing out presents. Mom and Dad make small talk as they hand all us kids our gifts.

Zayne got me a new, incredible leather journal. His parents got me some books about writing and autobiographies of journalists. Arriana got me a ticket to an online writing seminar and my parents got me an old school typewriter that makes me want to cry with joy.

Arriana bounces around as she opens hers. Zayne's parents got her some cute jewelry, I got her a couple new dresses, Zayne got her a rainbow throw pillow she's now in love with, my parents watch happily as she admires the beauty products and purse they got her.

We all pitched in to give Mr. Daveen his present. He got a check to help pay for new paint and parts for his station wagon. I don't think I'd ever seen him really roar with joy until then. I gave Mrs. Daveen a photo album of all of us kids, all the pictures we'd taken when we were still hiding. My parents got Mrs. Daveen a couple new cookbooks too.

My parents sit in awe of their gifts. My father loves his new monogram briefcase and ties, including one with a rainbow design. Mom almost tears up at the new set of pots and pans.

Carefully I scoot over to Zayne and hand him my gift. "Open it." I'm nearly vibrating from excitement.

He starts ripping the paper. I see the moment he realizes what it is. The way his whole body comes to life makes me feel like I did well. The Stitch onesie slides out of the paper along with the vinyl record of the Lilo & Stitch soundtrack.

He draws me into a kiss, muttering "thank you" against my lips over and over again. As he tugs on the onesie over his clothes, I see the equality necklace hang from his neck; instinctively I reach for mine. The cool black metal of the ring soothes me as it hangs from it's chain. By wearing these we've sworn to not get married until there is marriage equality for all.

Arriana's giggles remove me from my thoughts and back to my family. She and our parents are watching Zayne open another present.

He looks over the books he's been given, glancing up at Arriana with a chuckle.

"Josh told me you like to read so I went and found some cool new books. All the main characters are LGBTQ+."

I take note of some of the books, curious about them myself. He hugs Arriana and tells her how much he loves it. I see my dad out of the corner of my eye bringing out a large wrapped box.

Mrs. Daveen puts down her glass, scooting forward. "Ok Zayne, so this is from all of us. We all pitched in to get you this, even Tempe and Ciara contributed a little! Josh has already given you a bit of a hint."

Zayne looks at me, clearly confused. I feel the crooked grin form on my face as I watch him think.

We all watch him as he slowly unwraps and opens the box, I see the moment he realizes what it is. His shoulders slump and his eyes water. Our dads help bring out the record player and all the vinyls as Zayne sits trying to decide whether to laugh or cry. The record player also has a place to plug in his phone, and a CD player so he can listen to whatever he wants. He starts shaking and hugging everyone.

As we all coo over our gifts, Zayne sits in my lap and talks about the music he got. Arriana models all her new clothes and jewelry for us. I look at the cookbooks Mrs. Daveen got, we talk about the things we like best. Dad and Mr. Daveen talk about football and Mr. Daveen's car, he says he might paint it red.

Watching the family and community that's been built around me, I feel confident in the future. Zayne and I will never feel alone or isolated again, we have built a family of pure acceptance and love. Looking at Zayne I suddenly feel a weight lift off of me...

He will be ok. Bad days will happen, but we'll be here for him. I can't say I won't ever be scared for him again, but I also see that I don't have to constantly be in fear of losing him. He's not alone. *I'm* not alone.

His hand wraps around mine, yanking me back to reality. "Merry Christmas, Josh. I hope you liked your gifts."

Drawing his hand up to my lips, I give a sideways grin and kiss his knuckles. "I've got the best gift possible right next to me."

RITE OF PASSAGE

Time keeps moving forward, and Zayne keeps improving. It takes awhile for him to repair his muscles enough to play the violin again, but he does it and is playing by New Years. He plays all types of music including "No Matter What" by Calum Scott and "I Wouldn't Mind" by He is We.

Each time he plays I'm mesmerized, more so now that he's had to fight for the strength to play again. Watching him play, you can see how relieved he is to be able to do it again, the longer recovery took the more hope he lost of playing again.

Days turn to weeks, weeks to months, and we move past Valentine's Day when Zayne and I actually went on a real, nice date for a change. Easter comes along with chocolate kisses and real ones too.

The school year drags on and no one is ever caught or tied to the attack or the vandalism. Conrad never says a thing to Zayne ever again, no one ever speaks out against him, there are still dirty looks and anonymous notes and hate mail but nothing that can't be handled. Instead Zayne builds a bubble that people have become aware not to touch. Inside his bubble is me, Arriana, my mom and dad, his mom and dad, Tempe, and Caira, each of us ready to defend him at a moment's notice. His bubble stays impenetrable all year and he keeps getting better.

Prom night comes along, and I'm nervous. Arriana helped me pick my tux, she says I look fantastic but I still find myself vibrating with anxiousness.

"Why are you so nervous?" She chuckles as she adjusts my bow tie, her dress shimmering down her body.

"Just, I don't even know..." I reply. "I didn't think I'd ever go to prom, let alone with someone. I guess I'm nervous about what will happen. What if someone says something and it sends Zayne into a spiral?"

"His therapist is a phone call away if he needs it, plus he has you. He's not alone in this, Josh. We won't let him fight alone. We won't let *you* fight alone either. How are you doing in all this?"

I don't really know the answer to that. No one has really said anything to me, I get dirty looks and occasionally I'll get a note in my locker, but nothing like what Zayne went through. I still get scared sometimes, it wouldn't take much to attack us while we're on a date, or vandalize my house. It wouldn't take much to attack Arri for being related to me, or attack Zayne and put him back in his dark place.

I tell myself not to think about it. This is supposed to be a good night. It's supposed to be fun. Just him and me, not caring about anything but each other. Arri, Tempe, and Ciara are going as a group with us, and I'm looking forward to us all being together just having fun.

"Come on, let's not keep Zayne waiting!" She takes my hand and drags me through the house.

Mom stands waiting with her camera. Dad is behind her with a large grin.

"Stop right there! I want pictures!"

Arriana snorts as I try to escape, yanking me close and grinning at mom. "He was hoping he could get away without you bringing out the camera!"

Mom waves her hand dismissively. "Even if I hadn't taken any, Tiffany is waiting with her camera, too!"

Arriana draws me into a hug as we try to look good for the camera. Mom is giggling the entire time and telling me to stand up straight, my dad is silent as he watches us with a deep bellied chuckle, I can see a sparkle in their eyes as they tell us how wonderful and grown we look.

Mom starts tearing up as she waves her hands. "Alright, get out of here, go have fun...but not too much fun!"

I feel my cheeks get warm as Arriana chuckles at me. Dad tosses me the keys to his car as we walk out the door, I can feel my stomach fill with butterflies, I just don't know why, I know I shouldn't be this nervous.

"*Calm down, it's just a dance. Stop overthinking!*" I tell myself as I drive with Arianna in the passenger seat.

We pick up Tempe and Ciara before going to Zayne's place. Listening to the girls giggle and chatter doesn't calm my nerves. I feel my lip getting raw and worn as I try to bite away my nerves.

The drive to Zayne's apartment is short, but long enough to make my palms sweaty and my heart race. I try not to think as I park the car and get out with my sister.

"You look like you're going to be sick," Ciara visibly cringes at me as we approach the stairs. "Damn it, couldn't he live on the first floor, these are new shoes!"

I feel genuine happiness and excitement sneak into me and show on my face. "I'm sure as soon as Zayne hears your shoes are in jeopardy, he'll pack up and move!"

I earn some light giggles from Tempe and Arri, while Ciara gives me the finger. I'm still trembling, but my nerves calm a little. Letting the girls go ahead of me, I try to compose myself as they shimmy up the steps in their fancy dresses. I follow behind and wait as Arri knocks on the door.

Mrs. Daveen opens the door and gasps. "My Lord, you all look so stunning! Joseph get out here. You too, Zayne!"

Seeing Mr. Daveen walk into the room and light up, clearly pleased with how we all look, calms me some. Then Zayne comes out.

The moment I see him, I understand. I feel as the weight is lifted off me. All my nerves are gone as I realize why they were there to begin with. It's him. All the fear and anxiety comes from him, from being so lucky to have him, from being lucky enough to still have him after everything we've been through. My nervous energy comes from being so blessed as to have him in my life and him wanting me in his. It comes from knowing he's so amazing and I don't deserve him and knowing how easily I could have lost him. Seeing him now though, I know just how lucky I am, and how in love. Having him stand in front of me, the gentle, timid blush of his cheeks and sparkle in his innocent eyes. I see he's mine and that I will never want anything or anyone more than I want him.

His tie matches the pink tips of his hair, his gentle olive skin looks so bold against his simple black and white suit. Mesmerized, I'm unaware of my sister's light giggles and Mrs. Daveen bringing out her camera.

"Josh? Are you alright?" Zayne's voice is low and smooth as he takes my hand.

"Yeah," I snort at myself. "Yeah, I'm great. You look amazing!"

"Thanks, so do you." The blush in his cheeks intensifies.

"You look good, he looks good, Lord knows I look good!" Tempe wiggles her hips, making all of us chuckle. "Now let's hurry up or we won't have time to get dinner!"

"Not until I take some pictures! All of you get together and say 'Cheese'!" Mrs. Daveen points the camera at us and tells us how to stand. She gets a few pictures of all of us, some of just me and Zayne, some of the girls, and any other combination she could come up with.

By the time we finally get out of the apartment, even Arriana looks overstimulated. Zayne sits in the passenger seat next to me, arguing with the girls over the music on the radio.

"The alt stations will always have good music! It's not all punk and screamo, they play some of the pop songs you like, and at least it's not country!"

"What's wrong with country music!" Tempe looks appalled.

"Tempe, I'm pretty sure that your love of country music is the most unexpected and the only Texan thing about you, and let's face it, you just love Carrie Underwood's murderous tendencies." I don't fight the crooked grin on my face.

She purses her lips and wiggles her shoulders, avoiding eye contact. "If a man is going to be a pig, I think a few broken headlights are warranted."

"Just make sure you have an alibi. You'll say you were with

me crying it out over ice cream." Zayne and her exchange a look of understanding.

Ciara and Arri snort and giggle while I shake my head. "Heaven forbid you and I ever fight and break up. I'm gonna wake up to my house upside down."

"You two? Fight? Ha!" Arriana likes to think we're perfect.

Listening to the idle chatter, I keep my eyes on the road and Zayne's hand in mine. Arriving at Maria's Diner in town, we all fall out of the car and shuffle inside. The girls help each other adjust their dresses. Zayne and I stand there watching them, not really sure what to do.

"I don't really get it, I mean, they look fine," I whisper, begging Zayne for insight. He's learned a bit about fashion while hanging out with Arri.

He starts babbling about the girls' dresses and how they want to look nice but not accidentally flash anyone. Looking at me, he gives a gentle, humored grin and waves his hand, "It's a girl thing."

I look at him, totally lost. My confusion must be written all over my face as they all chuckle and he gives me a peck on the cheek.

"Arri is right, it's a good thing I'm gay. Women are complicated." My words have him cackling as we all make our way inside.

We're seated at the large booth in the corner, taking our time looking at the menus and joking around. Zayne and I decide to share a chocolate shake while the girls get their own. Occasionally we get up to take a couple of pictures in the retro style diner, or to play a song on the jukebox, but otherwise we focus on enjoying our food.

Arriana whips her phone out of her purse while I leave a tip and everyone else pays for their food. She tells us it's almost eight, meaning we need to get going.

The drive to the school is quieter, surprisingly. I feel Zayne's hand on my leg the entire way. He's nervous, I don't blame him, who knows what will happen.

No. It doesn't matter. Tonight is about us, about our friends. Tonight is about having fun. Nothing is going to ruin it. I won't let it. We all deserve a night to just have fun, and that's what we're going to get.

Parking in front of the venue, a nice hotel on the edge of town, we see large groups of kids dressed up like us. It's loud and crowded as dozens of teenagers shuffle into the ballroom.

Music floods our bodies, the beat thrumming through us as the lights flash,all of us grinning like idiots.

The girls are quick to squeal and disappear to the dance floor while Zayne and I stay close to the door, just taking it all in. I take his hand, luring him close to me.

"Did you ever think you'd be here?" He asks as he lays his head on my shoulder.

I shake my head, releasing a surprised chuckle. "Not in a million years, but I'm glad I am, and I'm glad I'm here with you."

He tries to hide his blush by enticing me into a kiss. Ignoring the dirty looks, we make our way to the dance floor, taking in the music and the energy around us. Nothing can compare to how freeing it was to just be for once, ignoring the negativity and enjoying being with the person you love. The joy so clearly evident on Zayne's face, as well as my sister's and her friend's, makes everything worth it.

Unable to help myself, I draw Zayne close, pressing his body to mine. My heart pounds in my chest as I feel the heat radiating from him, his lips twisting into a playful smirk.

"I fucking love you, you know that?" I run my hand down his cheek as I take in the sparkle in his eye.

"Of course, and I love you, too."

I keep him close as we dance into the night.

FAREWELL

Senior year feels like it's come and gone in a heartbeat. It feels as though my first kiss with Zayne was just last week, prom feels like it was just last night, yet here I stand watching my mom sob as she stares at me in my cap and gown.

"Mom, I'm not going to war, you don't need to cry." I feel awkward as my family stands watching my mom tear up and wave her hands.

"Ariel, we need to get going." My dad lays his hand on her tiny shoulder.

"No! We need pictures, it's not everyday your baby graduates high school," she argues, bringing her camera out of her purse.

I can hear Arriana giggling by the door. "Just wait Arri," I call. "This will be you next year, and you can't form-fit the gown or escape Mom's camera!"

I watch the color fade from her already pasty face, and I won't lie, it brings a smile to my face. The clicking of my mother's camera draws my attention. My mind wanders and takes me back through the past year, so much has changed and

I'm still in awe of everything that's happened and been accomplished. To think almost a year ago, I didn't even know Zayne, now I'm pretty sure I'll never love someone more than I love him.

Things could have turned out really differently this year. I could still be hiding, Zayne could be dead, but here we are, hours away from accepting our diplomas and saying goodbye to high school and this shit town.

"Josh!" My dad's voice snaps me back to reality, "You ready to go kiddo?"

Nodding, I follow them out to the car. My family chatters as the vibrations of the car relax me and the houses fly by out the window.

The school's parking lot is a mess, which isn't surprising, but it still puts my mother in a tizzy about being able to get through the crowds. Dad and Arriana stay with her while I go to line up with the rest of my class.

When I find my class, I push through the faceless mass of my classmates to find Zayne. It takes longer than I'd like, but I find him off in a corner with his parents.

"Hey." I breath out in a tired huff as I place my hand on his shoulder. "You ready?"

His parents beam at me. Zayne looks terrified. "This is really happening? We're really getting out of this dump?"

"Hell yeah, baby. Not even a week left, and we never have to come back."

A deep chortle escapes him as he draws me into a hug. His warmth seeps into me as I hold him. My heart pounds heavily in my chest as the music starts and we all file onto the field and into our seats, I can see Zayne a few rows ahead of me and listen as the speakers drone on.

Valedictorian, the principal, a guest speaker, I sit there bouncing my leg anxiously waiting. I don't know why I'm nervous. Is it normal to be this nervous? My palms are sweating and my chest feels tight.

One by one our names start getting called. One by one, I watch my classmates walk across the stage and collect their diplomas. I can hear both our families roaring with applause as Zayne crosses the stage, I can only imagine how adorable and red his cheeks are right now.

I don't clap as Conrad's henchmen cross the stage, and I won't pretend I'm not aware of the drastic volume difference when Conrad himself comes across. He has been pretty isolated over the past few months, after he flipped out and attacked Zayne and me he was threatened with expulsion and people started to realize just how twisted he was. Even if they don't agree with how Zayne and I are, they also realized Conrad had been taking it too far.

My nerves don't relax when my time comes to walk, if

anything I start vibrating more as I approach the stage. Carefully, I clench my fists until they hurt, hoping it will hide my trembling.

"Congratulations Josh, you deserve this." Mrs. Jennings' warm energy soothes me as she shakes my hand and hands me my diploma.

Sitting back down, I watch the rest of the ceremony in awe. I don't know how to explain the euphoria that came over me as I took my diploma.

"And now I present to you, the graduating class of 2019!" Mrs. Jennings' voice rings over us as well all stand and throw our caps in a frenzy of yelling and cackles.

We did it. We graduated.

"Are you going to miss it?"

I turn my head, watching Zayne push himself back and forth on the swing. His eyes rest heavily on the sky.

"Am I going to miss it? Miss what?"

"Waco, home, high school...all of it."

"I don't know. I'll miss seeing my parents and Arriana everyday. I'll miss our dates. You know I'm going to miss you."

He glances over, trying to hide his sad smirk by looking

down. "I'm going to miss you too. Is there no way to convince you to come to Seattle with me?"

"Could I convince you to stay in Texas?"

We both get a good laugh, we know neither of us want to be apart but we can't turn away from these schools. Zayne got an incredible scholarship and the school has great jobs at it's LGBTQ+ outreach center, and my school has an incredible writing and journalism program.

Both of us hesitate to speak or even really think about college. Fear fills us at the thought of what's waiting for us; neither of us really thought we'd get this far, we never thought we'd both be out of the closet and happily embracing who we are before we left. Neither of us thought we'd have someone special to leave behind, yet here we are, hand in hand, dreading being apart. Zayne leaves next week. He's been packing all week and he's been panicking just as long. We all worry about him being away from home, especially if he has another spiral, but we all know that this could be great for him. The community there is far more accepting and that's what he deserves, even if it means we can't see him as often as we'd like.

"Still scared?" I ask, reaching for his hand.

"I just...aside from that one winter break, I've never really left Texas. I'm nervous to be in a new place living with a random person without any of you guys."

"We're always a phone call away. You can always FaceTime us, and we'll both come home for the holidays. The distance won't keep us from loving you."

"You promise?"

I see in his eyes that he's just teasing at this point. Hauling myself up off the swing, I stand behind him, keeping him from swinging as I rest my chin on the top of his pink colored hair.

"Do you promise the same?" I whisper as I press my lips to his head.

"Of course. Always."

"Then so do I. I've got you, forever, unconditionally, and happily."

The next week flies by, and before I know it, I'm helping Zayne pack the last of his things and load them into his dad's car. We all come to see him and his parents off before they drive up to Seattle and help him settle into his dorm. They're going to drive to Utah before stopping at a hotel for the night and driving the rest of the way.

Arriana yanks Zayne into a hug, trying not to cry. "You promise to call and text? You have to send me your new address when you get there so I can send you stuff."

"Like you'd let me go without calling you," he says as he

pushes back. "I'm going to miss you, Arri."

She waves her hands as she looks away in an attempt to hide the tears. My parents take their turn saying goodbye and talking to Zayne's parents. My mom gives Zayne a couple tins of cookies to take with him.

As his parents load into the car, Zayne stares at me with wide eyes. He runs his hands down the side of his jeans before coming to hug me. He vibrates against me.

"You're going to be great, Seattle won't know what hit it." I draw him in closer, taking in every bit of warmth and using every second I can.

"I'm going to miss you."

His voice trembles. I try to hide how anxious I am for his sake. "I'm going to miss you too. Call me when you get there, ok? And hey, I'm always a phone call away."

"Boys!" Zayne's mom calls to us, her voice is gentle and low as she watches us with sad eyes, "It's time to go."

Before he has the chance to walk away, I take his face in my hands and press my lips to his. I want to remember this feeling, his soft lips and warm cheeks. I don't know when I'll be able to feel it next. His body softens against me. If I could, I'd never let go, and I almost don't.

Hesitating, we push away and watch each other for a

moment. I hold his hand as long as I can as he walks to the car. It's actually happening. He's actually leaving.

Part of me is still scared of him falling into his dark place again with no one there to bring him back. I have to trust he can handle it, and he'll have to trust that I'm here for him no matter how far the distance.

I watch him drive away and fight the tears as I turn to go back into my house and finish gathering my stuff to leave.

I tell myself it's not the end, that it'll work out.

It has to.

College Living

My roommate isn't here. Thank god. He's a nice guy but he's obnoxious as hell. I want to call Zayne, but it's hard to do that with my roommate screaming and playing video games every spare second. I'm a gamer too and at first thought he was cool, but god there's more to life than video games.

Sitting at my desk, I bring out my laptop and phone. I have an assignment due in four days; I have to write an article on a pressing issue in our world for my journalism class. Maybe if I'm lucky I can get a hold of Zayne and talk to him while I work.

Hoping he isn't at work or in class, I dial his number and wait. My leg bounces, causing me to flinch a few times as I hit the desk. It's probably all in my head, but I can't help but be nervous when he doesn't pick up.

"*He's probably working,*" I tell myself repeatedly.

I'm probably right. He works a lot to stay afloat, especially since he isn't close to home. He's not the only one who has work, but he feels more pressure to work long hours and earn more money, he doesn't want to ask his parents for help. I want him to take a break but he refuses.

"Hi! You've reached Zayne Daveen. I can't really talk right now, I'm probably in class, but if you leave a message or text me I'll try to get back to you soon. Bye!"

I release a defeated sigh as the long beep fills my ear.

"Hey babe, uhh, it's me. I just wanted to check up on you and see how you're feeling. You're probably working or in class, but if you could call me or text me when you get this...yeah. I love you."

I hang up, letting my phone fall out of my hand and onto my desk. It's probably nothing. I know he's just busy but I hate being away from him, and neither of us have been away from home this long. I'd be a fat ass liar if I said I wasn't this clingy out of homesickness.

My parents call every night, and while I love them, talking to them instead of seeing them reminds me of the distance. Huston isn't as far as Seattle, but it's still not home.

"*Focus, or you'll fail and be home before you know it!*" I tell myself as I turn back to my computer.

Research has to be my least favorite part of my courses, but I understand why it's necessary. Schoolwork is probably a blessing in disguise, forcing me to think of something other than Zayne and how far from home we both are.

I manage to write down a few ideas for my article when my phone rings. Jumping to grab it, I manage to fall to the ground.

"Hello?" I try to sound cool as I bite down and try not to whine in pain.

"Josh?" Arriana's voice fills my ears.

"God Arri, hi. What's up?"

"Nothing much, just checking on you. You doing alright?"

How am I supposed to respond to that? I mean, yeah I'm *ok* in the sense I'm not dead or dying, but I am exhausted and hungry and worried constantly. That's not even considering how I can't focus on anything because I miss being home. Does she need to know all this? No. Am I going to tell her? Of course.

"I don't really know, I just...I'm not sure. It's not as wonderful and liberating as you'd think to be at college."

"Are you not having fun?"

"No, it isn't that. College is great, it's just a really big adjustment, you know? Classes are different, assignments are new, it's weird being this far from home, and I...I just..."

"You miss Zayne."

"I miss all of you guys! I don't know, maybe it's just homesickness, maybe it's just because it's all new, but I wish I could turn back the clock and stay in that last week with all of us together."

"Well when you guys come home for Christmas it'll all feel normal again, and you can revel in it until you go back. Have you heard from Zayne recently?"

"Not in the last few days, both of us have really busy schedules," I glance at the time on my computer, letting out a groan. "I have to be at work in an hour, I don't know if I should nap or do schoolwork."

She asks about the assignment and helps me brainstorm ideas before we say goodbye and hang up. Why do I already feel drained, like just knowing how much work I have to do is dragging me down. I tell myself that the more I get done now, the more I can rest later.

"Just focus Josh," I whisper to myself.

Focusing isn't my strong suit currently, my mind still wanders to Zayne. I worry about him and his mental health and how people are treating him at school. The more I think of him, the more an idea comes to me.

Sitting back at my computer, I start typing to take notes for my research: *Effects of Intolerance on Mental Health in LGBTQ Youth.*

"Have a nice day!" I repeat for probably the millionth time

today.

"Do you need a break?" My coworker Trey asks as he hands another student a hotdog.

"Am I going to get paid for it?"

"No."

"Then there's your answer."

Rolling his eyes, he shoves me. Glancing at the clock, I see I still have another hour before I get off, I probably should take a break, maybe eat something. I could call my mom, or Zayne, take a minute to try and unwind, but I hate the idea of losing any time on the clock.

"You know, I think I will take a break. You good here for like 15-20 minutes?"

He nods as he focuses on not burning any burgers. I envy his ability to focus and work and be unbothered by anything.

Gathering my own food, I scan the cafeteria for an isolated table so I can call my family in peace. I know mom will pick up when I call, but it's Zayne that worries me. Knots fill my stomach as I stare at my food and listen to the long ringing in my ear.

"Josh, honey?"

"Hey mom!"

Her squeal fills my ears as a grin breaks out over my face. "Oh honey I was going to call you soon, how are you doing? Aren't you at work?"

"Taking a break, I wanted to check in on you and dad. How are you guys doing?"

"We're ok! Dad's out of town again, but we both miss you. Are your classes fun?"

Does mom need to know the truth of my exhaustion? Absolutely not. Am I going to tell her like I did Arri? Fuck no.

"It's great, yeah, I love my teachers and it's a lot of fun and a lot of my classmates are great. Work is kind of boring but I guess that's just life, isn't it?"

"Yeah, but it gets better. Once you find a job you love, work won't be so awful."

"I hope you're right. I don't know, it just seems like going through the motions: school, work, sleep, repeat."

"Make sure you find some time for fun honey, these next four years could be some of the best of your life, it's ok to take a moment and enjoy it. Have you talked to Zayne recently?"

"Not in the past few days, time difference and work and school make it hard. Both of us kind of expected that. We'll figure it out."

"Maybe I'll call his mother later, see if she's heard from

him?"

I know she's trying to make me feel better, find a way to let me know he's ok, but I just don't think she gets it. I've never been this far from home. I always miss everyone, I always worry about everyone, *especially* Zayne. Not getting to talk to him is a bit nerve wracking, but I don't want to seem obsessed or clingy so I just keep that all to myself.

"Yeah maybe, hey umm, Mom? I have to go, ok? I'll try to call you later."

"Ok honey, I love you. Try and rest soon, you sound so worn out."

"I love you too, Mom. Bye."

Putting my phone on the table, I let myself finally acknowledge and fall into the idle chatter around me. Giggles and yelling fill my ears as other students eat and talk about projects and crack jokes.

Now I wish I had gone to Seattle. Maybe I could go up there this weekend? Neither of us picked majors with any weekend classes. Maybe I could take Friday off from work and leave after my 3 o'clock class, drive as far as I can before resting a bit and booking it the rest of the way. I could be there by Sunday morning if not sooner, but that wouldn't leave much time for us to do anything together and getting back in time for school would be hell.

Pushing creative writing assignments and books and other junk to the side, I lay my head down on the desk. I debate whether or not I should call him. He'll text me when he gets my message, right? He's probably just really busy, I get that, I just wish I could hear his voice and make him cackle.

I'd kill to hold him, but I know that I can't do that and that waiting will make it that much better and exciting when I see him for Christmas. The time will fly, I just need to focus on something else, anything else.

Giving my phone one final death stare, I grab it. I'm vibrating with frustration as I shove the phone back in my pocket.

"Think of something else, anything else. Think about your paper... I wonder what Zayne would think of th—" I think to myself before realizing what I'm doing. *"Dammit! God I'm an idiot and a creep! Think of your food, think of your food and calm down. You're shaking, calm down and stop shaking... No, more like vibrating. Vibrating?"*

My pocket. I don't think it's me vibrating. It's my imagination, right? It has to be. I'm just tired and frustrated. I've heard of the Freshman 15 but is there anything like the Freshmen Frenzy? If not I might have invented it.

It won't stop. Could I possibly not be imagining it? I'm so hyper aware of the vibrations I can feel them in my teeth.

Reaching back into my pocket, I feel the vibration more. Someone is calling me. I wasn't going totally crazy.

"Hello?"

"Hey, there's the voice I've been missing."

My heart stops as his voice fills my ears, "Zayne." His name slips past my lips as I try to find words.

"Hi to you too." His laughter makes my body relax and melt into the phone.

"I miss you."

"I miss you too. Are you ok? You sound...off."

"Yeah, I mean no I'm ok. I just didn't think I was going to talk to you today, and hearing your voice, I just...God I wish I could see you."

"Well, my last class of the day got cancelled, maybe we could FaceTime?"

"Maybe, I'd really like that. Hopefully there's time for it. How's class?"

"Boring. I like the teachers and my coworkers, but the classes are a bit dull. There is this really good coffee shop by campus I think you would like, maybe you could come visit and I'll take you."

"I would love to come see you. Unfortunately I don't

think there's really anything new or interesting here I could show you, except... Maybe... My dorm? It's got a really nice bed." I can feel the smirk spreading over my face.

I swear I can hear the blushing from here, "What am I going to do with you?"

"Love me, like I plan to do with you. I'm really glad you called, I think it's just what I needed."

"I couldn't agree more."

We keep talking all through my break. I tell him about my article and he tells me what he thinks, letting me take notes along the way. He tells me about his course work and just what he's up to in general, even about a party he was thinking of going to with some coworkers.

Every second I hear his voice, I feel myself relax a bit more.

This is just what I needed.

2040

"I can't find it!" Zayne's voice rings down the hall.

"I told you, you left it on the nightstand," I holler back at him as I adjust my tie. "We're going to be late."

He runs down the hall to meet me in front of the mirror. "I'm coming. Stop fussing, your tie looks fine."

I look over at the wall behind us, all the pictures covering it. Covering all twenty years since we graduated and went off to college, neither of us sure we would make it.

I look at my hand to see the black ring wrapped around my finger, an exact replica of the ones on the necklaces all those years ago. It finally happened.

"Josh?" I look up to see Zayne staring at me. I miss the pink hair that covered the jet black. "Are you ok?"

"Yeah I'm just thinking about how we got here. What we had to go through."

He comes over and kisses me, his lips still as soft as they were the first time. "Stop thinking," he whispers. "We have to go. We need to pick up everyone and then get to the agency."

He starts towing me along to the door. He's so eager for what today means, what we've prepared all week for. What some could say we prepared all these years for.

Some years were harder than others, like the two years during college where Zayne and I weren't speaking because of a misunderstanding at a frat party, or the year Zayne got his job at the school LGBT+ support center and I got mine in my school's cafeteria and we never could get a hold of each other. Other years were easy, like the year Zayne encouraged me to self publish one of my short books, or the year Zayne and I moved back to Waco willingly and bought a house together.

It took a long time to build the lives we have now, from our house, to the home for displaced youth we opened a year and a half ago. While laws might change, people's opinions usually don't, so Zayne and I started a program that helps LGBT+ kids and teens who were kicked out by family. We call it Love Yourself Home. We offer a home, counseling and financial aid option to keep these kids in school. We're currently housing and helping eleven kids ranging in age from nine to eighteen.

It's baby steps like that and others in the country that showed politicians that the LGBT+ community is not the enemy and helped secure nationwide marriage equality ten months ago. Needless to say, Zayne and I made our way to a courthouse within a week.

Today we need to go to pick up Arriana and her husband from the airport, then pick up all the parents from their houses to bring them by the house. We have a major surprise for them.

Today, Zayne and I adopt a fourteen year old girl named Jessica. Jessica was supposedly a problem child who really had just lost hope after so long in the system, Zayne and I eventually got through to her and she asked us to adopt her.

So much has changed in the years and it sometimes boggles me. Conrad became a prominent business man here in Waco before he got married and moved to Washington D.C. Tempe got married in college and is still with the guy. Caira is still single and has become the vice principal of our old high school, and mine and Zayne's parents retired here in Waco and have since just relaxed and enjoyed life.

Waco has become far more accepting. Most of the country has aside from a handful of people. Now there's no fear of being attacked or abused while just walking down the street, instead, we've all come to see each other as what we are. Humans.

Zayne rushes to pick everyone and drop them off at the house. I tell Arriana to stall everyone for an hour, and like her normal self, she does so without question. I then replace Zayne as driver for safety reasons and we go to pick up Jessica. The way her face lights up when she sees us makes all the fighting worth it, all the years of fighting just to have this chance has paid off.

I look at Zayne and see the teenager in him again, the way his eyes light up and the way he squeezes my hand. He may have changed his hair and gotten older, but he's still very much the boy I fell in love with at seventeen years old.

We yank Jessica into a hug, her blonde hair flying everywhere as she accepts the embrace. We gather her stuff and load her into the car, ready to finally tell our family.

As we walk through the front door with Jessica, everyone looks stunned.

"Everyone," Zayne takes my hand and places his free one on her shoulder, we beam at each other. "This is our daughter, Jessica."

The room erupts in screams and cheers as everyone starts hugging everyone. We watch everyone approach Jessica to meet and talk to her, the smiles are contagious.

Zayne grabs my waist and jerks me close. "I don't know Josh," he looks at me funny, "I think Jessica will be lonely with just her and us. I think we should adopt another, a baby."

I chortle. "Ok, let's get her through freshman year first. Please, I beg of you."

Life is good. We fought our battles to make these moments possible and special. Some days we're reminded of our past battles, sometimes before bed when I see Zayne's scars I get taken back to that intense fear that I could have lost him. Some days when we go to the Love Yourself Home and sit in on the group therapy sessions, Zayne will hear a story that brings him back to high school and Conrad. Days like those are hard, but seeing where those memories got us takes a lot of the fear away.

Watching my family and friends greet the new addition to my family, Zayne lets go of my hand and runs up to the attic. He comes back a couple minutes later with a small bundle of tissue paper.

"Jessica," he calls her over and gets down on his knees to be level with the short teen, "This is something I've held onto for years. It was a gift from your dad when I was in a really bad place, they don't make them anymore. I want you to have it, I want you to have it as something to help bring you through your hard times and show you that you *truly are* a part of our family and our story."

She unwraps the paper and at the sight of what she holds, my heart skips and tears start leaking from my eyes. Jessica holds up a black T-Shirt that reads **Everything is Pride...And Equality Matters**. I watch the excitement on her face grow as she hugs Zayne tight. I go join them in their hug.

"Everything is pride, your pride holds your self-worth and the way you view yourself. Never let anyone tell you how to feel or tell you that who you are is wrong." Zayne looks up to me as he keeps talking to Jessica. "No one gets to decide who you are but you, and you need to *always* hold your head up and stay true to yourself."

She pushes away from the hug and starts thanking us, for adopting her, welcoming her, and the amazing gift. She runs off to show everyone.

"I thought you got rid of that sophomore year of college, after the frat thing." I grin at him,my heart skipping. I didn't think I'd ever see that shirt again.

"Actually, I wore it more after that, not having you those two years was really hard and that was my best substitute. Plus, nothing will erase how much that birthday meant to me. I very easily could have never *seen* that birthday. I don't take any part of it for granted."

I draw him in close to me and we watch our future continue to unfold in front of us, through our family, through the kids we help, and through our everlasting victory.

We were all in Jessica's place once, young and in high school. We all have been disregarding for who we are because who we are is different. Not much has changed since my high school years, but now we're working to change it.

We're finally free.

Bonus Content

Love Yourself

"This is the living room, we have a sort of group therapy once a week in here. It is optional, but we encourage it."

Looking down next to me, I see the young teen, the newest member of Love Yourself Group Home. Zayne will be here in an hour, we make it a point to be here for dinner with the kids at least one or twice a week. He'll be coming with Jessica once he finishes helping her shop for some new stuff for her room.

"Do you have any questions, Payton?"

Payton is 15 and came out as nonbinary and pansexual to their family a month ago. Their family kicked them out, and this is their third home.

"Where's my room?"

I try to give a welcoming smile as I help them with their bag. It's a trash bag, the standard for foster kids. I can't imagine it helps their self esteem.

"It's upstairs. You'll be with Denis. Come on, I'll introduce you and then we can sit down and talk some more, ok?"

They nod, keeping their arms close to themselves as they

walk. The home is fairly large, Zayne and I spent a good three years raising money and building. The second and third floor are just bedrooms and bathrooms so the kids have space.

Making our way up the stairs, I take Payton to the last door down the hall. Knocking gently, I feel my heart flutter and try to give a reassuring grin as I meet Denis's bright eyes. I try to remind myself they all start out like Payton, and that we just can't give up on them.

"Hey Mr. Josh, what's up?" Denis bounces over to the door, looking at us both.

"Hey kiddo, this is your new roommate, Peyton! I figured you two could meet and you could help them settle in before dinner."

Denis looks at Peyton with excitement.

"Absolutely! I'm Denis!" I watch Denis drag Payton gently into the room. "I'm bisexual, my pronouns are he/him. I've been here a month now and I think you'll love it here! And you came at the best time, all of June Mr. Josh and Mr. Zayne have all this fun Pride stuff planned!"

I keep my eye on Payton as I stand in the doorway, it's a lot to take in and I don't want them to get overwhelmed. They stay calm, but their eyes are darting around.

"Hey Denis, why don't you go show Payton the game room in the basement. Maybe you could pick a movie for tonight if you want. How about it, Payton?"

They shrug and make their way with Denis out of the room and to the basement. Reminding myself that healing takes time, I wander to the kitchen. I'm pleased to see our main caretaker, Mariah, and a few of the other kids goofing off.

"Mr. Josh!" Our youngest member, nine year old Tiffany jumps off the counter to come hug me. "Mr. Josh, come help! Miss Mariah said we could make cupcakes!"

"I hope that's alright," Mariah looks up at me as the corners of her mouth tip up and she waves the whisk in her hand. "I figured, we could have them at movie night. Tiffany and Greg insisted on all the sprinkles, but don't worry they weren't expensive!"

My chuckle vibrates up my throat. "Don't worry about it, it'll be fine, what's a few dollars, I can cover that." I look at all the different colors the kids have, most are organized to look like the different pride flags.

"Will Mr. Zayne and Jessica be here soon?" Our newest trans member, Greg asks as he licks some frosting from a spoon.

"In about an hour I think. Jess needed some new stuff for her room and I think they might bring some stuff for movie night. Have any of you guys met Payton yet?" They all shake their head, but look interested, a new member is always interesting. "Just try to remember how scared you all were when you came. Let's try to welcome them and make them feel safe."

Tiffany grips my hand. I can't imagine any of these kids want to remember where they started. Tiffany got kicked out because she and a classmate were caught kissing and holding hands on the playground. Greg bought a binder and his mom threw it in her fireplace before trying to beat him. Even Mariah came from a questionable place. She used drugs to try and "bury the lesbian" as her family put it. I just hope they can all find happiness.

The silence is deafening. Bringing in new kids means old kids facing what they've been through, and I hate seeing them in pain, but they're safe and that's why we have group therapy. In an attempt to lighten the mood, I bring down some of the sprinkles from the cabinet.

"Tiff, why don't you take some of these and get the other kids, we can all decorate together."

The hesitant grin comes over her face as she runs off with the sprinkles. Greg steps closer, standing stiff. He's turning 18 in a month and has been here for over a year. He still struggles when remembering his parents.

"You doing alright, bud? It's alright to be upset." I pat his shoulder.

"I just don't get it. I don't think I ever will. How can our parents say they love us one day, and then say they hate us when they find out we love differently, we're still their kids!"

He starts quaking. Gently holding his shoulders I whisper in his ear.

"You're safe now. It's ok. You are safe and loved and valid. We're here for you, we will fight for you. It's ok, you're safe. It's ok to not be ok. Not everyone will understand, not everyone will accept it, but they have no control over you. Remember how strong you are, remember how loved you are, remember you are not fighting alone. You are safe, you are loved, you are valid. You are not alone. Remember who you have fighting in your corner, you are safe. Take a deep breath."

He squeezes my hand on his shoulder until his knuckles turn white. The pain is like needles, but it's probably nothing compared to what Greg is feeling. His breath is trembling, I can hear him trying to slow his breathing.

"Mr. Josh?"

Glancing up, I see Tiffany, Denis, and Payton. They look scared. Nodding to Mariah, I watch her take them into the living room and away while I calm Greg.

"Talk to me bud, what can I do? What are you feeling?"

His voice comes out a low whine. "It hurts. She hates me, she keeps calling me a monster, she says I'm a horrible daughter, and that I will never be her son."

"Greg, listen to me, she can never hurt you again. She doesn't deserve you, losing you will be one of her biggest regrets. She will never see what an amazing man you will become, she'll never get to see how big a heart you have. She won't hurt you again, you're safe." He finally opens his eyes, revealing how red and wet they are. "Remember the exercise we learned last month? You want to do it together?"

He nods, "Can-- can you start it?"

"Five things you can see. I see sprinkles, the fridge, Mariah's granola bars, your phone, and the oven."

"Th-- the cupcake tin. The umm, the frosting, the whisk, Tiffany's water cup, and my shoes."

"Four things you can smell. I can smell dinner cooking, and the cupcakes. I also smell Mariah's perfume, and the laundry detergent smell from downstairs. I think I also smell cologne."

"Yeah, I smell all that too."

"What do you feel, what are three things?"

"Your hand, my jeans, and uh, the cold counter."

"Two things you hear?"

"You and the kitchen timer."

"Ok, now what's one thing you can taste?"

"Frosting."

I lighten my hold on him. "Ok, now take a deep breath and come back. You're safe here."

He's still shaking but he doesn't stand as stiff. Grounding is something we've found to be helpful for him and some of the other kids, to help bring them back to reality when they get trapped in those memories.

Carefully I take him out into the living room, Mariah is sitting with Denis and Payton and Tiffany, they all watch with concern. Sitting Greg down on one of the lounge chairs, I make my way to Mariah and the kids to make sure they're ok.

"What was that?" Payton asks, they are visibly disturbed by what they had witnessed.

"We all have some memories we struggle with, but that's why we're here. We all come here to find the love and acceptance we were denied, we all will learn to face those memories."

"Do you have any memories?"

Mariah takes a deep breath and looks up at me. She knows Zayne and I's memories, she's been here long enough to hear us discuss it in group with the kids. Mine are arguably much smaller next to Zayne's but we both still struggle.

"Yeah kiddo, yeah I do. I remember being attacked and told to go to hell for defending myself and the person I love. I remember what they did to him and tore him down right in front of my eyes. I remember months of horrible notes being shoved in mine and my sister's lockers because of who I am. Those memories will always be there, but we learn to deal with them in time and use them to grow and fight back."

Payton looks stunned. If I had to guess, they feel the way Zayne and I felt when we realized we weren't alone. "What do we do to help when one of us gets like this?"

My lips stretch into a grin. It's comforting that Payton wants to help and considers themself one of us. "Usually, it differs for all of us. For me or Greg, grounding and reassurance and time are what help. For Mariah it's always been cooking."

"For me it's drawing, drawing what I'm feeling and getting it out of my head calms me." Tiffany raises her hand.

Payton looks at us all for a second before rising from the couch. Shock is evident on all of us as they waddle across the room. They look uncomfortable, but determined with their tall stance but timid steps.

"Hey," they whisper to Greg, "Can I sit here?"

Greg glances up, looking through Payton. He's still coming down, but he nods and makes room for Payton next to him.

"I'm Payton."

"Greg."

"I really like your shirt. I love that band." Payton points as

Greg tugs his shirt down showing the name *Paramore*.

"Yeah?"

"Yeah, Brick by Boring Brick was amazing."

Greg watches Payton closely, trying to focus. "Yeah, umm, Monster...Monster is my favorite."

My shoulders relax as I watch them. The two of them talk, slowly relaxing into each other's company. Denis goes and joins them and the talking quickly grows into roaring laughter.

As more of the kids come downstairs or come home from their part time jobs, if they have one, the house settles. Greg is still shaken but finds comfort in being with the others.

Since opening the Love Yourself group home, we've had over 30 kids come through. They build a family here, we help them find themselves and find support. We help them find jobs and get scholarships. Events are held year round to bring them into the community and raise money for the home so we can give them a normal happy life. Many of the kids still call and write letters from college and the homes that adopted them. Knowing we truly help these kids makes the years of fighting and all the struggles worth it.

Mariah comes to stand next to me as we watch the kids all talk and meet Payton.

"I wish I had found a place like this when I was their age." Peace fills her voice. "You do a good thing here, you're giving them the fresh start they need."

"No."

She looks back at me, her eyebrows furrowed and lips turned down.

" *We* give them a family."

Cupcake Palooza

L aughter fills the yard as children run in circles. I can see Zayne over by the bounce house collecting tickets, all of the Love Yourself Group Home kids are walking around with buckets or are sitting at different stations in the yard.

Today is the last day of our Pride Weekend Palooza. We spend the entire last weekend of June every year celebrating Pride and raising money for the home and the kids.

Zayne sees me and grins. I glide over to him, drawn to him and his happy energy.

"Serious turn out this year." He says as he takes another ticket from a young child and lets them in the bounce house.

"Upside to working at the newspaper, advertising." A chuckle escapes him as I bring him in close and look around. "The kids all seem to be having fun, and this could be great for them and the home."

We have some of our older kids like Jim and Kathrine working at the barbecue with Mariah, while the younger kids like Tiffany and Sasha play and sell raffle tickets.

"The number of volunteers is incredible, it will never cease to amaze me how a community can come together for its kids."

I see Payton, Denis, and Greg hanging out with Jessica over by the face painting station. We were lucky the high school's art teacher saw our ad and volunteered her time, the face painting is a big hit. I see all four of the kids with different pride flags painted on their faces.

"Jess seems to be getting along with them. They all seem to be settling in really well."

"Have you introduced Payton or Denis to any of the potential families? I know Greg talked to a couple, so did Sasha, but I haven't seen those two meet any."

"They might not be ready. It's hard to trust after what they've been through, you know that just as well as I do."

"Of course I do, I just... I want them to find what we found. Everyone deserves a family."

"Zayne, they do have a family. We're helping them build one here, it may not be conventional but then again neither are we."

His cheeks turn a gentle pink as he looks away. His attention returns to the bounce house as I look over the yard. Young couples talk to the kids, social workers talk with couples, families run around with their kids. The line for face painting crosses the yard, the grill and bake sale are full of excited conversation, and the line for the bounce house hasn't shortened since we opened this morning. People walk around the raffle table excitedly, and I can't blame them, we didn't have this when we first started but a lot of local businesses and some friends donated some stuff for us to raffle off to draw in a crowd and sell tickets and it seems to be working.

I can see Tiffany and one of the other kids her age, Mark, talking with one of the potential adoptive families. They both try to look cute and sell a number of tickets. A couple of real entrepreneurs, those two, I feel a laugh bubble up inside me as I watch.

"Mr. Josh!"

I turn to see our oldest child, Marsha, coming over to me. She looks excited.

"It's time to announce raffle winners, and we've sold almost all the food we have!"

"We may have to close up early, but now we should be able to help pay for you to go to grad night!"

"I can pay for that Mr. Josh, you don't have to do that!"

I see the glitter paint shimmer on her cheek, the bisexual pride flag in the form of a butterfly moves as she talks.

"We want to help you, that's why you're here. I like the butterfly by the way."

Touching it delicately, she chuckles, her cheeks turn pink around the butterfly. "Thanks, I thought it was appropriate given I'm going to be a senior, after this year I spread my wings and age out of the system."

"You've done research on scholarships for schools you're interested in? You made sure your boss will give you a good reference?" She nods as I pat her shoulder. "Promise to always remember that this is your home, and we'll always be here for you? You can always come to us."

"Thank you Mr. Josh!" She wraps her arms around me in a tight hug.

I chuckle and wave her off. Grabbing Zayne's attention, we cross the yard to the large tables covered in prizes.

Marsha hands me a crappy microphone that's tied into our equally crappy speakers. Watching the guests wander about, we turn down the music and collect the raffle buckets.

Tiffany comes up with a stray raffle ticket, "Can I put it in the Easy-Bake oven bucket, the one with the cute purse and chefs hat?"

I hear Zayne giggle behind me as he passes the bucket to Tiffany and lets her drop in her ticket.

"Alright, if I can have everyone's attention! It's time for the raffle and the announcement of our total money raised."

People start to form a small crowd around us, watching eagerly. Zayne comes to stand next to me, trading the microphone for the raffle bucket.

"As many of you know, Josh and I grew up here and Waco, and we along with others have fought for this for years. We've come so far in these past 20 years. Now couples like Josh and I can live in peace and start families, but it is still a battle. We still face problems with displaced youth, children pushed aside by intolerant families. With your help we give them a chance and help them find themselves here at the Love Yourself Group Home. I'm happy to be here announcing our raffle winners and thanking them, and those who donated prizes, for their contribution to helping us rebuild these young lives. So, before I bore you all to sleep," He chuckles with the crowd. "First prize is a dinner date for two at Vers Le Ciel, we have..."

I dig my hand into the bucket, finding and taking out a ticket. I check to make sure it has a number and name as Zayne points the microphone at me.

"Our first winner is Jennifer Manson, number 3938110. Is Jennifer here? Jennifer Manson?"

We watch a hand in the back of the crowd shoot up. One of the kids goes to get their information to give them their prize at the end of the raffle.

This process repeats through the course of ten more prizes. Toys, books, electronics, event tickets, one by one they are claimed. Tiff didn't win her raffle but she takes it in stride. I tell her to just keep it in mind around Christmas time and she may get lucky.

Arriana wins a prize, new pots and pans for her kitchen, but she wasn't able to come tonight so I decide to hold it for her to pick up tomorrow. Zayne and I are meeting her, her husband, and Ciara for lunch tomorrow. Tempe is out of town otherwise we'd invite her. It's been a while since we were all together and I won't lie, I miss it. I miss all of our adventures over the summer and building the trust and friendship we came to have.

As all the prizes are collected, one of our volunteers, the high school math teacher, calculates the money we've made from the whole weekend. Raffle tickets for a dollar, two dollars for food items and drinks, five dollars for a meal, three dollar karaoke station, tickets for face paint at five dollars, three dollars for a trip in the bounce house, ten dollars for Love Yourself Group Home shirts, fifteen dollars for hoodies. Hundreds of each item sold, I'm confident, and that's before the donations we've received. Dozens have donated their time, prizes, and money to help us.

Zayne takes a piece of paper from the volunteer, stepping up beside me with the largest grin I've ever seen.

"This year, with your help, we have managed to raise $6,457.60 for our home and to better the lives of these children!" Applause erupts around us as we draw each other close and giggle with excitement.

I can see all the kids standing together, watching in disbelief, I can see Denis tearing up while Marsha hugs Greg. Knowing that their community came together to do this for them must be an amazing feeling, especially after what they've been through.

Mariah takes the kids inside while the rest of us start to clean up, still in awe of all we accomplished. Zayne and I sit on the house steps staring at that little piece of paper showing over $6000 that we'll be putting into the home and into bettering these kids. We sit and talk about all the good it will do, Christmas gifts, being able to pay for college applications for the older kids, new school clothes and supplies, and so much more.

Today has been...incredible.

"No! No, that's not it, it's *how* he said it that was funny." Mariah snickers as she mimics a man from her old job, triggering the kids to laugh with her.

I help the kids dish out food in the kitchen as we all sit down for dinner. The kids are all in high spirits and have been cackling and beaming since the end of the fundraiser this afternoon. We held a group therapy meeting after everything was done, just to check on the kids, and to hear how loved they felt when they saw their community fight for them was such a huge step. Even Payton spoke and seemed excited, and they've had a hard time adjusting.

"What made you get into this line of work, you know, like foster care and stuff?" Jessica sits next to Denis, Payton, and Greg as she looks at Mariah.

"This, this is what got me doing this. Seeing these kids, seeing the family we were building and realizing how badly I needed it growing up and how badly I wanted to help."

Zayne takes my hand as we sit at the table, flowing into conversation. Marsha and Kathrine talk about work and getting ready for senior year, Jim talks about wanting to be a senior too. Tiffany and Sasha rave about the bounce house and beg us to bring it out again, I tell them we might. Our other kids talk about what all we could do with the money we raised, of course, being young they come up with crazy ideas. One boy, Rory says we could go to the moon!

"We love you kids, you know that?" Zayne bursts out, bringing a calm silence to the table.

"And we're glad that this weekend could show you how loved and special you are, and show you how worthy of that love you are."

They all nod and light up, grinning from ear to ear, some reaching for each other's hands as they watch us. Tiffany drags

Sasha into a hug, both of them blush and tear up.

I grab my glass and lift it above my head, "I just want to tell you all how proud we are. You've all overcome a lot, and being here has definitely come with its own struggles. I want to make a toast, to another great year! To new beginnings. To friendship, to equality, to love, and most importantly, to family."

"To family!"

All around the table, glasses rise above us and laughter erupts again as the kids start talking again.

Zayne leans over, pressing his lips to my cheek, along my jawline. Sending chills up my spine, I try not to react to much while the kids are here. I soften at the sight of his gentle grin as he runs his finger over my wedding ring. Giving my hand a squeeze, he whispers something as he turns to the large table again.

"To love and change."

ACKNOWLEDGMENTS

There are so many people I'd like to thank, so many people who made this book possible. Starting with, to me, the most obvious, my dear friend Simon, who pushed me to be myself always and pushed me to show the world this truth of being LGBTQ+ even in this day and age.

I also want to thank all the people who showed me this was possible, without an agent or publishing agent and that I could do this at such a young age. Thank you to the other self published authors who helped me through this journey. Thank you to Anna D. Stoddard who helped me figure out each step, Sophie Elaine Hanson who encouraged me and is the greatest editor I could have ever asked for. Thank you to Catherine Downen who helped me understand all the options I had and showed me how to flaunt my book as the magnificent piece of hard work it is. Thank you to Trinity Lemm, Lee Jacquot, Bella Grace, Lane Northcutt, Denielle Keil, Cheyenne Bluett, Hannah Cowen, and so many other self published authors who stood by me and encouraged me and gave me friendships to lean on during this process.

Thank you to my friends Hannah of The Paperback Bookclub, and independent musician Miggie Snyder for always finding ways to support me and help me get my name out there. Thank you to all the people who were reading and supporting this story when it was nothing more than a 19 chapter mess on Wattpad. Friends like Elle, Elektra, Noran, Eden, Alyssa, and all the other dear friends I found through Wattpad, I can't imagine where I'd be without you! Thank you to my wonderful friend Grace, who works so hard to help me get my name out there, there couldn't be a better friend and social media manager.

Thank you, finally, to my family. Not just my blood family, but to those who chose to be my family. To Mrs. Laura Byington who encouraged my writing, to Ms. Afsaneh Safaie who was always there when I needed her, Mrs. Mia Bertelsen, Ms. Alicia Began, and Mr. Bayless for always having kindness and wisdom to share. Thank you to Ms. Riana Bucceri, Mr. David McBean, Mr. Matthew Stover, Mrs. Jenny Moore, and Mr. Brad Couture for always encouraging my personality and creativity, you all gave me a family outside of my home. Thank you to my mom and dad who worked hard to keep me safe and take me away from a really toxic environment, thank you for being there and fighting for me no matter what.

Thank you to everyone who has and will buy this, you have helped prove every doubter wrong, you've proven that dreams come true. Thank you to everyone who is struggling but chooses to stay with us, we know it's hard and we see you, and we will stand by you. Thank you to everyone who embraces themselves, and fights for themselves and others, you're valid and loved.

ABOUT THE AUTHOR

Born and raised in Southern California, Kat Winters discovered a love of writing at a young age. Now 19 and living in Missouri, Kat hopes to touch others through her writing and help others and provide gripping stories.

Kat also loves photography, cooking, baking, reading and so much more. Creativity and giving have always been strong parts of Kat's life and she hopes to give people the same escape through reading her books that she found writing them.

Kat tries to focus on inclusivity in her books, as well as bringing attention to real problems in our world. She always strives for a good story that will hold a reader and make all feel welcome and heard and engaged. She supports all people and is a firm believer in "be unapologetically you" and only has intolerance for toxicity, hatred, and bigotry.

Kat hopes to become a teacher, a foster mom, and a writer who works to connect to all types of people from all different circumstances and make them feel included.

Any and all readers and supporters are loved and appreciated unconditionally for who they are and how they help Kat achieve her dreams.